DIRTY SWEET WILD

WILD

JULIE KRISS

Also by Julie Kriss:

Bad Boyfriend
Bad Wedding

The Bad Billionaires series:
Bad Billionaire (Book 1)
Rich Dirty Dangerous (Book 3)

Chapter 1

Max

I WOKE UP ON THE STRANGEST DAY OF MY LIFE WITH A
hell of a hangover. I don't usually drink—I got out of
the habit when I was on the meds—but for some reason
I'd tied one on the night before. Whiskey. Consumed while
sitting home alone on my sofa. Just another Monday night
in Max Reilly's rundown apartment, in the chilly fog of San
Francisco.

My head fucking hurt. I didn't have a shift today, at
least. I worked construction for cash under the table, usually across the bridge in Oakland. You'd think I wouldn't
be prime material for a construction worker—my leg sees
to that—but you'd be wrong. I had no problem getting on
crews. Today was a day off, though, and I rolled out of bed,
cursing Last Night Max's idiocy, put on my leg, and made
my way into the kitchen, wearing only boxer shorts.

Coffee and toast didn't help much, so I cleared out
the rest of my hangover by going to the gym. The rain had
cleared out and I could see the dark clouds rolling off over
the bay as I drove the short distance through the south end

1

of the city to Sporty's, the gym which was practically my second home. It was cheap, and a hole in the wall, and it smelled like unwashed balls and dirty socks, but no one asked me questions there. I'd never seen a woman there, ever—a woman would have to be nuts to go to Sporty's—and the guys were all as silent and surly as me. It was the kind of place where you could lift weights at three o'clock in the morning on the nights you couldn't sleep, and you wouldn't be the only one there.

By the time I finished at the gym, the whiskey had mostly sweated its way out of my system, and my head was only throbbing at the temples. I put down the weight I'd been lifting and lay on the weight bench for a minute, staring at the water stains on the ceiling.

This was my life: my shitty apartment, my gym, my shifts in the dirt on construction sites. Drinking alone at night and trying to pay off my medical bills and my dead father's debts. I liked it this way—no complications, no women, no one bothering me. All I'd wanted since the day I got home from Afghanistan was to be left alone. So, yeah, this was my life.

Except it wasn't.

I had five million fucking dollars in my bank account.

Damn Devon Wilder, my best friend. He'd inherited big time from the grandfather he'd never known, and the next thing we knew, the friend I'd grown up dirty on the streets of LA with was a billionaire. He'd also met a woman he was flat out crazy about and would probably marry, if I knew him at all. And because he was Devon, and because he knew I was drowning in the debts I owed, he'd wiped all of them away with one big deposit into my bank account.

It was the best, most generous thing anyone I knew had ever done. It changed everything. I owed him my life.

I felt like I was falling.

I made myself take a breath as sweat broke out on the back of my neck. My chest felt tight. *Shit, shit. Keep it together, Reilly.* I closed my eyes as the world spun and my stomach clenched. This wasn't the aftereffects of the whiskey. No sir, this was pure, one hundred per cent crazy-as-fuck Max Reilly and his shitty brain.

I waited. I took breaths. I pictured a path in the woods, crisp air, fall leaves. I went to that place and stayed there for a while. Then, when the attack had passed, I got up and went home.

It was nuts to have a panic attack over what most people would see as a dream come true. But it was the change that my messed-up psyche couldn't handle. My entire life, such as it was, had been upended with one bank deposit, dumped out like laundry tossed on the floor. I had no idea what the hell to do. It made my thoughts scramble when I tried to think about it, because I'd already been through a lot of crazy shit in my life. So I kept doing the same old things to make myself feel sane—and sometimes, when I wanted to stop thinking, I apparently drank whiskey like an idiot.

I showered for nearly thirty minutes, holding the handle I'd installed in the shower stall, letting the hot water run off my body. My spine felt tight and weird, and my leg ached. I put on jeans and an old t-shirt and my leg again, then I made a sandwich in my kitchen and forced it down into my screwed-up stomach. The anxiety had receded, but it had left me clammy and shaky, like I'd just had the flu. So I did the thing that usually worked for me—I grabbed a book from my bookshelf and sat down to read.

My bookshelf was overflowing, one of the biggest things in my tiny apartment. I liked to cruise used bookstores—there were a few left in San Francisco—and add to my collection, the stranger the better. I hadn't always been a reader; I'd grown up running wild on the streets, my mother barely home, my father usually drunk. It was only after I'd enlisted that I really discovered how reading made everything bearable. Long plane rides. Endless nights deployed. Long, dead stretches of time in the desert. And, later, the time I'd done in hospital after hospital, the time stuck in waiting rooms and in bed recovering from surgeries. I may be crazy as fuck, but I could guarantee I'd be even crazier if I hadn't found the outlet of reading.

The book I had now was *The Call of the Wild*, a yellowed old copy with a screwy green cover that didn't even have a wolf on it, even though the book was about wolves. It had cost me two bucks, and it was very fucking good. I absently massaged my leg and sat on the sofa, letting the book take me away.

I was so engrossed that I almost didn't answer the knock at my door.

The first thing I thought was to ignore it. Who the hell knocks on a guy's door at three o'clock in the afternoon? No one good. Someone selling something—no thanks. Nosy neighbor, wanting to bitch about something—no thanks. Cops—no thanks. The landlord—no thanks. I didn't owe any back rent, thanks to Devon Wilder.

But the knock came again, and I put the book down. Now I was distracted. I stood up and limped across the room, reluctantly opening the door.

Holy shit.

It was a woman. Not just any woman—a fucking gorgeous woman. She had light blond hair, and blue eyes in a sweetly heart-shaped face that also featured a soft, sexy mouth. She had makeup on—dark eyelids, dark lashes, lip gloss. She had perfect skin and elegant hoop earrings that brushed against her flawless neck. She was smiling at me, but her mouth naturally had a fuck-you attitude to it, an I-don't-give-a-shit twist that made you think of sex. Just like that. One look at her face, and you thought about fucking. Fucking her. Fucking anybody at all.

I dropped my gaze. She was posed deliberately, her weight on one hip, her long legs displayed. She had a handbag over her shoulder and a coat on. A trench coat-type thing, belted at the waist. It only went to mid-thigh, and beneath it was nothing but miles and miles of bare leg, as if she wasn't wearing a single thing underneath it, finishing in heels that were inches high.

"Daniel Parker?" she asked.

I was dumbfounded, so completely shocked that a single word tripped out of my mouth. "What?"

She brushed past me and walked into my apartment, and I realized that she'd taken the word as agreement. I turned and stared at her as she put her bag down on a side table like she owned the place, and then she dug through it. She pulled out a little square and put an iPhone on it, fiddled with a button.

"This is from Andrew," she said. "Happy birthday!"

The music started. Pulsing, sexy music. The blonde stepped forward, and her hands went to the belt of her trench coat.

And that was when I realized she was going to strip.

Chapter 2

Max

THERE ISN'T MUCH YOU CAN DO WHEN A WOMAN walks into your apartment and starts stripping, except stand there and watch.

She tossed her hair and sashayed toward me, her fingers toying with the belt of her coat as I stood there, staring. I could have opened my mouth, told her that I wasn't the guy she thought I was, that it was all a misunderstanding, but then she put a hand to the middle of my chest and gently pushed me backward, aiming me for the sofa. Her hand shot a bolt of fire through me, woke up parts of my body I hadn't even known were asleep. My blood pulsed hot. I moved back like I was hypnotized, going wherever she wanted me to go.

When the backs of my legs bumped the sofa, I sat down. She stood just past my knees and played with the belt again, and the unreality of the situation washed over me. *Holy shit. She's going to take that thing off. She's actually going to do it.*

I shouldn't let her. But I couldn't stop it. And suddenly I really, really didn't want to. Vaguely, the last of my moral dignity reminded me that that made me an asshole. Then she undid the belt and dropped the coat, and my moral dignity shut up.

Under the trench coat, the blonde was wearing a skin-tight black dress with a zipper up the front. The dress was so low-cut that her tits, in some kind of miraculous push-up bra, nearly spilled over the top of it. The hem of the dress ended barely past her ass. As the music played on and she did a slow, sensuous little wiggle, I could pretty much see every inch of the body beneath the thin fabric. And it was a body like I'd never seen in my life.

Those big, soft, generous breasts. A slim waist, ending in a flare of hips. Long legs. Heels. She turned around and bent slightly, giving another sensuous wiggle of her hips, and I was glad I was sitting on the sofa, because the heart-shaped ass she showed me was out of this world. I'd woken up in my normal life, hung over, and suddenly I was living a perfect male fantasy. It had walked through my door and bent over practically in my face.

There was no way I was telling her she had the wrong man.

The music pulsed. She looked back at me over her shoulder, biting her lip. It was all a show, and a good one. Whoever this Daniel guy was, his buddy had ordered him a top-of-the line stripper. He'd spared no expense. She turned back around and moved closer, brought the show up a notch. She edged in between my legs, bumping my knees. I let her, forgetting for the moment about how my jeans covered a leg she likely wouldn't want to look at. Fuck it. I hadn't seen a naked woman, a real one who wasn't on the internet, in four years. *Four fucking years.*

She leaned forward, put her hands on the back of the

sofa behind me. Now she had me caged, her knees pressing into the sofa between my legs, her body held over me. The pose put her cleavage right in my face, her breasts practically brushing my beard. I put my hands on my thighs, where my palms sweated into my jeans, and took a breath. Coconut body lotion, hair spray, and sweet, slightly sweaty woman. I closed my eyes, unable to take it for a second. I had never smelled anything half as good in my life.

She did a sensuous snake-like move, slithering her body like she was nearly humping me. I wanted to put my hands on her hips, pull her down onto my lap, but I didn't think I was supposed to do that. You weren't supposed to touch the girl, right? I couldn't remember. My brain wouldn't work.

She answered the question for me by picking up one of my hands from my thigh and putting it to the top of her zipper. Then she did the snake move again, making what was left of my blood move straight into my dick. "Go for it, big guy," she said, her voice hot and throaty, the kind of voice you wanted to hear in your ear moaning *fuck me, God, fuck me harder* as you pounded into her as hard as you could.

I pinched the tag of the zipper between my fingers and looked up at her face. She had her long lashes lowered, looking down at my hand, but when I paused she raised her eyes to mine. And she looked straight at me.

Something happened. We both froze for a long minute, our eyes locked. Hers were a soft blue color, almost gray, and beneath the makeup and the heavy mascara they were observant, intelligent. They were also fixed on mine, and as we stared a pulse of confusion crossed them, though she didn't look away. Then her pupils dilated, slow and black. Her lips parted. And still she looked at me.

I couldn't breathe as I watched her back. I could feel everything—the spot where her knee pressed the inside of mine through my jeans, the electric brush of her breasts in the black dress, the cold zipper between my finger and thumb. The music disappeared behind the roaring pulse in my ears, and suddenly I realized it had stopped. We'd been staring at each other so long that the song was over.

In the silence, I could hear her breathing. I could hear my own. She blinked, still staring into my eyes like she couldn't stop. A lock of hair fell over one eye, blond and perfect. Her tongue darted out and she licked her lips.

I didn't know what was happening. I only knew my ribs felt like they were about to crack. I had every muscle tied down so tight that my whole body ached. I could feel my own pulse in my neck. I tore my gaze away from her eyes and glanced down at the zipper I was holding.

"You want me to do this?" I asked her, my voice hoarse.

She hitched a breath, and I saw her breasts move. Her tongue darted out again, briefly, touching the middle of her top lip, like she was imagining how I tasted. When she spoke, her voice wasn't theatrical anymore, not the sexy tone she'd used before. Instead it was barely a breath.

"Do it," she said.

I didn't need another invitation. In one quick motion I unzipped the dress from top to bottom, letting it fall open. She lifted her arms from the sofa behind me and shrugged it to the floor.

Now she was wearing only a skimpy black lace bra and matching panties. Her body was a revelation, her stomach flat, her hips perfectly round, her thighs long and strong. And those breasts—there was nothing unnatural about

9

those breasts. They were nothing but soft flesh, barely contained by the confines of the tiny bra, the nipples darkly visible through the lace. And those nipples were hard as chips of ice.

I raised my gaze up to hers again, and something arced between us so strong it took my breath away. She wasn't doing a show anymore; there was no more music, no more script. Instead she kicked off her tall heels in two quick motions and straddled my lap, her knees on either side of my hips, her hands on my shoulders. I put my hands on her hips—they were warm and so fucking soft—and pulled her down onto me. Then I lifted one hand to the back of her neck beneath her hair, pulled her down, and kissed her.

She didn't even hesitate. She kissed me back, pressing that sexy mouth into mine, parting her lips, letting me take the lead. I tried to take it at least a little bit slow, like I wasn't a goddamned animal, and I almost succeeded. I explored every corner of her mouth, my beard scraping her skin, my teeth and tongue scraping off every last trace of her lip gloss. She made a soft little moaning sound as I did it, and then she opened wider and slid her tongue into my mouth, and it was on.

I held her still and kissed her with everything I had in me, and she gave it right back. We were locked like that for God knew how long, her hands moving into my hair, her mouth wild on mine. My other hand pulled her hip down, pressing her against my throbbing cock in my jeans, and she cried out at the contact, biting my lower lip. Then she moved, rubbing up slowly against me like she couldn't help herself, and kissed me harder.

I was going to fucking explode. I broke the kiss and

moved my mouth down to the tender spot at the corner of her jaw, down her beautiful white neck, scratching her tender skin. She tilted into me and her hand curled tighter in my hair, holding on. "Oh, fuck," she said, praise and a curse at the same time, like she couldn't quite believe what was happening any more than I could.

I sucked gently at the spot where her neck met her shoulder, making her squirm against me helplessly, and my hands traveled to the middle of her back, unhooking the black bra. She gripped me harder with her knees as I dropped the straps down her shoulders and her breasts came free.

She didn't let go of me, and the bra drooped between us, still looped on her arms. I slid my hands up under it and cupped her breasts, staring in fascination at the way my big hands swallowed them, the way the flesh moved in my palms. She sighed, and I looked up to see she'd closed her eyes and tilted her head back, lost in the sensation. It was then that my fucked-up brain remembered that I had something to tell her.

So, with her spread-kneed and mostly naked on my lap, my cock throbbing, my hands full of her incredible tits, I made myself say it, though my voice wasn't much more than a rasp. "My name isn't Daniel Parker," I said. "It's Max Reilly. You got the wrong apartment."

I thought maybe she'd flinch. Back away. I was giving her the chance.

But she stilled for only the briefest second, taking in my words, before she let out a breath. She opened her eyes, leaned forward again, and grabbed my face with both hands.

"You know what?" she said. "I don't fucking care."

Chapter 3

Gwen

THERE ARE CERTAIN THINGS I JUST DON'T DO ON THE job. I don't let anyone touch me, ever. I don't do one-on-one gigs—they're too risky compared to the usual parties, and the tips aren't as good. And I never, ever, *ever* fuck a customer.

Somehow, today I was going to break every one of those rules.

I took the job today for the same reason I do anything—I was restless, a little bored, in an impulsive mood. When I get this way I usually kill it by taking my clothes off, so I called up Candy Cane and asked what was on the roster. They had this gig. Some guy ordering up a stripper for his buddy's birthday gift. It was better than nothing, so I took it.

And now I was on the wrong guy's lap, naked except for a scrap of lace between my legs, my knees gripping his hips, my breasts in his big hands. And I didn't want to leave.

How did I get here? I'd noticed him from the minute he opened the door. It was hard not to—he was big, with a dark brown close-cut beard and mussed dark brown hair. Sexy.

Not my usual type—I prefer well-groomed guys, clean shaven, well dressed. A guy who knows his way around an expensive restaurant menu and which is the best kind of wine. This guy had a kind of animal charisma to him, more like a guy you'd find somewhere deep in the woods, and he'd be a lumberjack chopping wood, and he'd see you and he'd drop his axe and he'd bend you over, and then he'd—

That was how it started.

I'd met Devon Wilder, my sister's new boyfriend, and he was one juicy steak of a man, but this guy was different. His muscles were bigger, like he lifted weights. He was wearing a t-shirt—washed so often the cotton was thin, the neck stretched over one perfect collarbone—and worn jeans over his muscled legs. His biceps were works of art; women have wet dreams about biceps like that. The right one featured a tattoo I couldn't quite see, snaking out from the sleeve of his t-shirt. He squinted at me like I'd interrupted something, and his voice was rough like he didn't use it often. He looked warm and powerful and slightly grumpy, and I wanted to push him down to see if he'd push me back.

But this was a job, and I'd done my act, trying to do it like I always do. So what if I was attracted to a customer for the first time ever? I could get in and out, escape this big bear of a man without embarrassing myself. No problem. Until I had him pinned on the sofa, doing the move that every guy likes, and I looked into his eyes.

When they get a strip show, most guys like it, but it embarrasses them, too. They laugh to cover it, or they wave their hands—*okay, okay, fine, get this over with*—or they roll their eyes. The shyer ones cross their arms and clam up, waiting for it to be over while their buddies laugh and clap. The real showmen whoop and holler and do a little dance move, like we're putting on a show. I'm used to all of it. Whatever, as long as I get paid.

This guy didn't do any of that. He just sat on his sofa, his hands palm down on his thighs, his expression intent. His gaze ate me up. His chest rose and fell. And when our eyes met, I saw *everything*. I saw that he was smart and fascinated and turned on. I saw that he was unaware of how hot he was. I saw that he had some kind of sadness, deep behind his eyes, that had nothing to do with me.

And I saw the raw fact that he really, really wanted to fuck me. Hard. And he was keeping himself in check.

You want me to do this? he asked, his hand on the zipper of my dress.

The words went through me like wildfire. I was close enough to catch his scent, the tempting smell of male skin, close enough to feel the heat radiating from his body and hear the rasp of his breath. And I wanted him to rip my clothes off.

So I told him to. The music had stopped. When I got on his lap, his heat was like a furnace, making me shiver, and his hand fit my hip perfectly. He kissed me exactly the way I was craving—deep, dirty, a little bit rough, like he wanted to devour me. My skin sang everywhere he touched me. I could feel his cock hard in his jeans, rubbing just so against my clit when I pressed my hips into his, the sensation making the blood pound in my ears and even harder between my legs. That. I wanted that. Inside me, right now.

He undid my bra and cupped my breasts, his thumbs brushing over my nipples, and I didn't care about his name. I didn't care about my own name. I cared about raw, primal, no-holds-barred sex. With him.

I told him I didn't care, and then I kissed him again. He kissed me back, his hands squeezing me, and then one hand dropped between my legs, into the scrap of my panties, his fingers sliding into the friction between him and me.

I made a noise and moved my hips, grinding on him slowly. I was so wet I slid easily over him, the pressure slick and perfect. He was breathing hard, watching me. His other hand left my breast and moved up to the back of my neck, where it wound in my hair, his grip strong. I closed my eyes, the pleasure sparking through me. I could come like this, just on his hand. I could make myself come so easily. But I wanted more. I wanted everything.

As if he was reading my mind, he pulled me down so his mouth was against my ear, his hand still on my pussy. "I am going to fuck you so fucking hard," he growled.

I nearly came with just that. "Do it," I panted, nearly frantic. "Do it."

He pushed me off his lap, tossing me so I was on all fours on the sofa. I gripped the arm as he yanked down my panties, and then I felt his weight shift as he got on his knees, heard the click of his belt and the zip of his jeans. And then he gripped my hips with both hands and thrust inside.

I dropped my forehead to the sofa arm, closing my eyes. It felt so good. He was big and powerful, stretching me just right, and I was so wet he just slid in. He stilled, then moved out of me slowly, then back in again. I wiggled, pressing my ass back against him.

"Fuck," he said when I did that. "Give me a second. Just—*fuck*," he said when I did it again. "Hold on, woman."

"Harder," I said, opening my eyes.

He leaned forward, over my back, braced himself on one big arm, that magical, sexy-ass bicep right next to my cheek. His other hand stayed on my hip. "You'll get what you want," he promised, and then he started to move.

I closed my eyes again and made myself breathe. Bliss. It was pure, absolute bliss. I moaned and melted into him, and slowly we found a rhythm, my body in sync with his. It was slick and perfect, and we made the sofa creak, then thump as we moved harder. I felt his mouth drop to the back of my shoulder. "Fuck," he said again.

"Don't stop," I told him.

He didn't, but he slowed—I practically cried—and dropped the hand on my hip down and around, between my legs, pressing gently against my clit. The friction was just what I needed, and I felt my body arch.

"Faster," I told him.

He bit my shoulder gently as he felt me move, felt how close I was. "Nope," he said.

I moaned and dropped my forehead to the arm of the sofa again, closing my eyes. I was so close I wanted to scream at him. I was used to having control. *You don't know how to do it. What you have to do is—*

And then I was coming, the orgasm wrenching through me, making me cry out. He rode me through it, dropping his hand from my clit and going faster, harder, until he stilled and came, groaning deeply into my hair. I took a deep breath and realized that I had never had sex that felt this good in my life. Not ever.

That was how I met Max Reilly.

Chapter 4

Max

I'D SPENT HUNDREDS OF HOURS IN DOCTORS' OFFICES—
the medicals for the Marines, the emergency surgeries,
the endless work on my leg. That wasn't even counting
the shrinks' offices I'd been to. I'd never been in a single one
that was comfortable.

I sat on an exam table in my boxer shorts, my legs dan-
gling over the side, my leg off, my hands braced on the table. My doctor, a gray-haired woman well over sixty named
Helen, was making notes on her clipboard.

"Can I put my clothes on now?" I asked her.

"In a second," she said without looking up. "Everything
looks pretty good. How's the leg?"

I didn't look down at it; I knew what it looked like. My
leg was gone just below the knee, part of my shin and my
foot vaporized by an IED in Afghanistan four years ago.
Now I wore a prosthetic, a metallic thing with tendons and
a foot, like something the Terminator would walk on. "It's
great," I said. "Fucking fantastic."

She didn't bat an eye at my tone. Helen was used to me.

After our first argument when I'd started coming to her two years ago, she'd told me to call her by her first name. "Any pain?" she asked.

I shrugged, my shoulders tight. Shit, it was cold in here. "A little."

She glanced up at me. "You want something for it?"

I shook my head. "No meds."

"Okay, fine. Are you doing the stretching exercises?"

"Yes." I did them at the gym every day.

She looked at my leg again. "You've been taking care of it. The skin doesn't look irritated. The scars look good."

"No, they don't," I countered. "They look like my leg was blown off."

"Well, aren't you in a grumpy mood today?" she said, my shit mood bouncing off her. "Something sure crawled up your butt. When was the last time you saw your counselor?"

I looked up at the ceiling. The fact that she never took any of my shit was the reason I still saw Helen. That, and she was one of the few people I actually talked to. "I'll probably start going again."

Her lips flattened into a disapproving line. "You stopped?"

"I ran out of money."

She paused. "But now you haven't run out anymore."

"No." I thought of the five million dollars in my bank account. No, I was no longer broke. I just felt like I was.

"So you're going to make an appointment with Dr. Weldman," she said, pressing me. "Right?"

I sighed. "Right."

"Today? I can pick up the phone right now."

"I can do it." I looked at her face. "I *will* do it."

"Thank you. You can put your clothes on now. Is there anything else?"

I grabbed my t-shirt and pulled it over my head. "There's one thing."

"What is it?"

I looked at the ceiling again, feeling the burn of embarrassment crawling up my neck. "I need a blood test."

Helen looked through the forms on her desk. "We can do that. What for?"

I cleared my throat. "STD's."

She had found the form, and she put it on her clipboard, her eyebrows rising. "You plan to become sexually active?"

She knew the deal, because doctors always ask that shit, no matter how humiliating it is to answer no. That was me. No. Four years of no. Now I had to humiliate myself even further. "I already, um, was."

She blinked at me. "Max, are you telling me you had unprotected sex?"

"Maybe. Sort of. Yes."

"With a man or a woman?"

Jesus. Could this get any worse? "A woman."

"Okay. And are you in a relationship with this woman?"

I couldn't admit that I didn't even know her name. She'd never told me, just gotten dressed and walked out the door. *See ya*, she'd said. That was it. *See ya.*

"No," I managed. "No relationship."

"But this woman was on birth control, right?"

I scratched my beard. "Well, I assumed."

Helen's eyes went wide. "Oh, for God's sake," she said. She scribbled furiously on the blood test form. "I'm used to lecturing eighteen-year-old boys about this, not twenty-nine-year-old men."

I closed my eyes briefly, wishing Hell would open up and swallow me right now. "You don't have to lecture me."

"Apparently I do." She tore off the form with a brisk swish and handed it to me. "Take this," she said, "and pray. Also, get in touch with this woman and ask for a medical history. Ask her to do a pregnancy test in three to four weeks."

Right. I was going to call the strip-o-gram company and ask for the number of their hottest blonde, in case I knocked her up two days ago. "Fine," I said, to get Helen off my back. I slid off the table and put my leg back on, then my jeans.

By the time I'd tied my shoes, she had rifled through her doctor's cupboard of goodies and turned back around to me. "And for God's sake take these," she said, handing me two big handfuls of condoms. "And use them."

"Jesus, Helen," I said, looking down at the dozens of condoms in her hands. "What the hell? I'm not going on tour with a punk band."

"Just take them," she said, shoving them at me. I took them and pushed them in my pockets, the plastic packets sliding together, trying to slip out again.

"These will last me until I'm ninety," I grumbled, stuffing them deeper into my pockets.

"Good," she said. "Now get out of here, Casanova, and get your blood drawn."

* * *

An hour later I was at the Shop-Save, paying for my groceries. I'd gone there almost without thinking, even though the Shop-Save was shitty, a little grimy, and depressing. Force of habit. Five million bucks in the bank, and I was still going to the same old places.

I pulled my wallet out of my pocket, the bored cashier looking on, and a cascade of condoms fell onto the floor.

Well, that was just fucking great.

The cashier, a girl of about nineteen, couldn't suppress a snicker. The woman behind me in line wasn't as amused. She was carrying a two-year-old boy, who was crowing and reaching his hands out, trying to get down so he could investigate the condoms on the ground. The woman gave me a look that said I was pretty much on her shit list.

I bent down and picked the condoms up, shoving them in my pockets again, my leg aching as I got down on the floor and then back up. The cashier was still smirking as she handed me my change. "Jeez, you're popular, huh?" she said.

I didn't answer. I just took my bag of groceries and left, limping a little now. I was done. This day was done. I had nothing else to fucking say.

In the driver's seat of my car, I pinched the bridge of my nose, trying to get myself together. "You dipshit," I told myself. It seemed incredible to me now that the sexiest blonde I'd ever seen had actually walked into my apartment two days ago. That she'd stripped for me. Looked at me. Touched me. Kissed me. That she'd practically begged me to fuck her, and when I had... When I had, it had been something. It hadn't been awkward or weird or out of sync. She had fit against me like we were two puzzle pieces, and she'd come so hard I'd *felt* it. It had been fucking perfect.

Right now, it felt like it had never really happened.

I ran a hand through my hair, then drove back to Shady Oaks. My apartment complex dated from the sixties, and it was built like an old-school motel, a low building circling a central courtyard, the stairs and the corridors open to the sky instead of enclosed. In the center was a dried-out pool that no one had used in decades, now full of dirt and leaves. It was far from downtown, and it was cheap, and my neighbors were mostly dirtbags and low-level criminals of some kind, but that was fine with me. It meant that no one ever bothered to be neighborly. Devon had passed his apartment to me when he moved out into his big house in Diablo, and now the place was mine.

I climbed the stairs, my grocery bag perched in the crook of my arm, and headed down the open corridor to my door. It was afternoon now, brisk, the sun winking in and out from behind the moving clouds. I raised my gaze and stopped.

The blonde was standing in front of my door. She was dressed different this time—jeans, a t-shirt beneath a loose dove-gray cardigan. She'd traded out the stiletto heels for flip flops. Her arms were crossed over her chest as she watched me.

I paused for a second, taking her in in shock, and then I started walking again. Her gaze flicked down over me, noticing my limp. I always got this way when my leg got tired.

I came closer and looked down at her. She raised her eyes up to mine, and I saw she had no makeup on—not a trace. Her hair, which was just past shoulder length, didn't have any hairspray in it, and it blew softly in the breeze. In the sunlight, completely naked of makeup, her face was even more beautiful than before.

See ya, she'd said, and she'd let the door close behind her.

"Hi," I managed.

"Hi." She bit her lip. "I need to talk to you."

I blinked. I couldn't imagine what she had to talk to me about, but then I remembered Helen and her lecture. "I need to talk to you, too."

She shrugged. "Okay."

I put my key in my door and let her in, then walked to the kitchen to put my groceries down. I turned to find her standing in the middle of my apartment, her fingers hooked into the pockets of her hip-hugging jeans, looking around as if she'd never seen the place before.

"You have a lot of books here," she observed.

I snorted a laugh. "You didn't notice that last time?"

"I guess not." She swiveled slowly, looking around, and it was all I could do not to bark at her, ask her what exactly she saw. Did my place look pathetic to her? Like the apartment of a guy who lived alone and never got laid?

I banged my groceries a little hard on the counter, because I was nervous, and she jumped. Deciding it was best maybe not to scare the shit out of her, I slowed down. I turned my back and discreetly emptied my pockets of the annoying fucking condoms, tossing them in the silverware drawer. Then I made myself walk calmly around to the other side of the counter and lean on it, watching her. "What do you want to talk to me about?" I asked her.

She suddenly looked uncertain. I had never seen a sexier woman. It came off her like a scent, was in every way that her body moved. Even though she wasn't dancing, even though she was in a roomy t-shirt and sweater, her long legs encased in worn jeans, her painted toes in flip-flops, she was ridiculously, naturally sexy. I had no idea what the hell she was doing here.

She didn't answer my question, so I said, "Since you already know mine, why don't you start by telling me your name?"

She lifted her chin and her gaze snapped on mine.

"It's Gwen," she said. "And I came to tell you I'm not a slut."

Chapter 5

Gwen

T HE WORDS JUST HUNG THERE, LIKE WE COULD BOTH see them. *I am not a slut.* Well, fuck it. I'm not. And for some reason I couldn't figure out, it was important to me that he knew.

The guy—Max, his name was Max—looked genuinely surprised at that, then his brow furrowed. "Okay," he said. "I never said you were."

I rolled my eyes. "I'm just making it clear, okay? I know what I do for a living, what it looks like. What it looked like when I was... here." I blew out a breath. "You might think I do that all the time. But I don't, okay? I've never done anything like that before."

He crossed his arms over his chest, and the motion made his biceps look like something you'd put in a porn made just for women. He was looking at me, not with judgment, but with a soft sort of curiosity. "I didn't think you were a slut," he said. "I didn't think you did that all the time."

"No?" I scoffed. "What did you think I was, then? A stripper who shows up and fucks her customer?" I made the words sharp, hurtful, because that's what I do. I bring the hurt before anyone can bring it to me.

But Max just shrugged his big, hot shoulders. "I just thought you were a woman who wanted to be fucked," he said, his voice rough. "And you didn't fuck a customer, by the way. Someone hired you, but it sure as hell wasn't me."

It was the most words I'd heard from his mouth, and his voice gave me a shiver. Low, rough. *I just thought you were a woman who wanted to be fucked.* He had a voice made for saying words like that.

I tried not to stare at him curiously. His place was tidy and clean, but it was obviously the apartment of a guy who lived alone and didn't go out much: a TV, all those books, a set of hand weights in one corner, a laptop, a kitchen that was obviously stocked. I didn't see any sign of a woman anywhere—no decorative bowls or nice paintings or tossed-aside clothes—and I hated how badly I wanted to know if my guess was right.

"Well, don't worry," I said, keeping my gaze away from the sofa, where he'd bent me over with that big body and practically made me scream. "I just had an itch, that's all. A one-time thing. I can get sex anytime I want."

He looked slightly alarmed. "You don't have a boy-friend, do you?"

"God! *No,*" I said. "Jeez. Do you have a girlfriend?" *If you don't answer me, I swear to God I'm going to search your bathroom for her tampons.*

"Fuck no," Max said. "I think you can guess that from the way I practically jumped you."

Now my cheeks were warm. That was two firsts today: Tracking down a guy because I was worried about what he

26

thought of me, and getting embarrassed talking about sex. "I didn't mind," I admitted, understatement of the year.

He scrubbed a hand over his face, rasping it over his beard, then ran it through his hair. "Okay," he said, avoiding my gaze. "I have to ask you. Are you on the pill?"

Once again, the words hung there, along with the idea of this huge man impregnating me. *Holy hell.* But of course, he didn't know. "Not only yes," I told him, "but *hell* yes."

He nodded, and his shoulders relaxed a little. "And have you been checked out?"

"You mean blood tests?" I put my hands on my hips. "Of course. You think I gave you something?"

"Gwen," he said, "I didn't even know your name until ten minutes ago."

I stared at him, sent off-balance by how my name sounded in his mouth, and then I got myself together. "Well, I don't have anything. Maybe you gave *me* something."

"I didn't," he said.

"And how do I know that?"

"I can show you the paperwork," he said. "I've had dozens of tests. I just had another one done this morning, if you want the latest."

Dozens of tests? What did that mean? I'd noticed him limping when he came down the corridor toward his door. *Jesus, Gwen, he's just a guy you fucked. Stop being so curious.* "Okay," I said, taking my hands off my hips. "I'm sure it's fine. Just… let me know the results."

"You want to give me your number?" he asked. When my gaze flew to his, I watched his expression shut down, become carefully blank. "I'm not going to hassle you."

And it struck me: He was shy. That was what the

gruffness and the growling were all about. He was big, and he was hot, and he was smart, but the shyness was practically crippling him. I took my clothes off for a living, and I liked bold, confident men—men I liked controlling, cutting down to size. I'd never wanted a man anything like Max, but I'd already fucked him, which I made most of the men I dated wait months for. Max Reilly was shy, but not when he had his dick in me.

No, I didn't usually like men like Max. But right now I did. And I could have any man I wanted, right?

I reached in my pocket and pulled out my phone. I stepped closer to him, close enough to look up at him. "I'll give you my number on one condition," I said.

Now there was wariness behind his careful blank expression, like I was going to make him do a test. "What condition?"

"You use it to ask me out."

I waited. Most men would be pretty fucking happy with that condition. I turned down guys all the time. All. The. Time.

But Max just looked at me with those dark eyes and said, "No."

I felt my eyebrows go upward. "No?"

"No," he said again, and when he saw the look on my face, he elaborated, "That's not a good idea."

I'll be honest, it took me a second to process that. Maybe that makes me seem like a jerk, but I was a blonde stripper with an absolutely perfect body, thank you very much, and this guy was saying no with sort of a regretful tone, like he was letting me down easy. "Why is it not a good idea?" I asked.

I thought maybe he would mumble something, try and

get rid of me, but instead he looked at the ceiling for a second, putting his words together. Then he looked back at me and scowled. "Because a date leads to more sex."

Now my jaw actually dropped open. "You don't want to have sex with me again?"

He scowled harder, as if I'd said something crazy. "Of course I do, for fuck's sake. It's just that it's a bad idea."

I crossed my arms over my breasts. "You don't get out much, do you?" I asked him.

He didn't answer, which meant no.

"Here's how it works," I said, as if he'd spoken. "You're single. I'm single. We're both free, and neither of us is gay. I'm on the pill, and we've established we don't have any diseases. So we go on a date. We have a few drinks. We talk, or something, and when you take me home, I give you a blow job. See? Simple."

"Oh, my God," he said. He looked at the ceiling again, and I realized I'd turned him on. *Oh, hell yes.* I dropped my gaze down his body while he wasn't looking, taking in that chest, that stomach, those sexy worn jeans. I'd tossed the words out, but now that they'd been said I realized I wanted in there. Bad. I was literally trying to get into this man's pants. What was wrong with me?

Max reached out and took my phone from my hand. "Give me that," he said, his voice short. Yes, I'd definitely turned him on. He opened the texting app and texted himself so he'd have my number. "There will be no date," he said grumpily, "and there will definitely be no blow job. Are we clear?"

"Why not?" I asked sweetly. I liked cranky, turned-on Max; he was amusing. I batted my lashes. "I'm very good."

He made a pained sound and shoved my phone back at me. "Trust me, you don't want any part of me."

It was like he was leaving these openings on purpose; no way was I letting them pass by. "Just *one* part of you," I said, holding up a finger and giving him a sexy smile. "That's all I ask."

He shook his head. "I swear to God," he said. "What is it going to take to get rid of you?"

"Tell me the truth," I said. "It isn't because I'm not hot, and it isn't because you don't like me. So why?"

He blinked at me, and it looked like he made a decision. "You really want to know?" he asked, and when I nodded, he said, "Fine."

He reached down to his belt and unbuckled it. I felt my eyes go wide as he undid his jeans and dropped them, right there in front of me, letting them pool on the floor at his feet.

I stared. He was wearing navy blue boxer shorts, but that wasn't what I was looking at. My gaze traveled down, where his right leg ended below the knee, and the rest of his shin and his foot was a metal prosthetic. The leg, the real one, was twisted with scars—old ones, long healed, but so profound it looked like a shark had taken bites of his flesh a long time ago. My first thought was, *My God, that must have hurt so fucking much.*

I raised my gaze back to his face. His expression was blank again, carefully composed, the expression that meant this was practically killing him. "What happened?" I asked.

"Afghanistan happened," he said, his voice stripped of any emotion. He watched me steadily and gave nothing away. "An IED happened. I came home with this, and with a case of PTSD that nearly killed me. You get it now?"

Chapter 6

Max

"THAT SEEMS LIKE RATHER AN EXTREME reaction," my counselor said. "Dropping your pants for a woman you barely know."

"I guess," I said, staring intently at the wall. "It seemed like the right thing to do at the time."

We were in his office, a small, stuffy room in a boxy medical building in the wasteland of South San Francisco, far from the trolley cars and the nice Victorian houses. Like Shady Oaks, this was the kind of place tourists never saw—full of ugly industrial buildings, cheap apartments, and occasional vacant lots. My therapist's name was Dr. Weldman. He was a black man of about fifty with dark-rimmed glasses and a demeanor that was very fucking calm, which had been helpful during the many times I'd pretty much fallen apart at the seams.

But I was calm today. I was in an uncomfortable chair that was a little too small for me. I'd turned it so I wasn't facing the doctor, but instead could look at the wall, which was easier when you were talking about embarrassing shit. Dr.

Weldman never minded when I turned the chair. He probably didn't want to look at me either.

"Still," he said, pursuing the subject of Gwen and my fucked-up meeting with her in my apartment two days ago. "It isn't your usual mode of behavior, even under stress."

"She wanted to go out with me," I said. "She needed to know all the shit that was wrong with me first. I was doing her a favor."

"Or perhaps you were hoping to scare her off."

I turned my head and gave him a brief glare. "I was *counting* on scaring her off."

He nodded. They always nodded like they'd already expected everything you said, these therapists. I'd gotten used to it long ago. "And why do you think that is?" he asked.

I looked at the wall again. "Like I say, I was doing her a favor," I said. "She probably shouldn't have anything to do with me."

"Because you believe you're not worthy of her?"

It should be a stupid idea. She was a stripper—who wasn't worthy of a stripper? But it wasn't a stupid idea. At all. "I don't know about worthy," I hedged. "I just know I'm a fucking mess."

"You're not as bad as you used to be," Dr. Weldman said softly. "And you'll be even better if you keep coming back to see me regularly."

"Yeah, well, I'll see what I can do. Maybe I can clear my busy schedule."

Like Helen, Dr. Weldman was used to my pissy moods, and they never seemed to affect him.

"You said you started coming back to your sessions

because you came into some money," he said. "Tell me about that."

The money. I didn't want to talk about the money. It was going to make me feel sick again. But shit, that was why I was here, right? "My friend Devon inherited a lot of money."

Dr. Weldman nodded. He knew all about Devon, since he knew my life story, and I'd known Devon since I was six. "I take it he shared some of his good fortune with you?"

I made myself say the words. "He shared five million of his good fortune with me."

There was a pause, and I wondered if I'd surprised him. He didn't let on. "You seem tense when you say that," he observed. "Many people would be pleased."

I shrugged. "It's more than I'll ever need. More than I ever expected."

"So it's a sudden change, then. I see. What did you tell Devon when he gave it to you?"

"I told him to fuck off and take it back." I looked at the ceiling. "Some friend I am, right?"

"I'd say Devon sees you as a perfectly good friend," he said, with so much reason I wanted to punch him in the mouth. "He wouldn't give five million dollars to a terrible friend. I'd say he sees something in you that you don't see in yourself."

I shook my head. I didn't want to know what Devon saw in me—what anyone saw in me. "He thinks I'm an asshole," I said. "And so does this woman, especially since I showed her my leg."

"Did it work?" he asked.

"Did what work?"

"Scaring her off by showing her your leg. Telling her about you."

When he put it that way, it sounded like Gwen and I had had a nice heart to heart. "She just kind of shook her head," I said.

"And? Did she say anything?"

I sighed, reluctantly dredging up the memory. "She said that it was a miracle, but she finally found someone more fucked up than she is."

There was a moment of silence. Dr. Weldman cleared his throat. "And how did that make you feel?"

I shot another glare at him. "You're laughing. You think that's funny."

His face was blank, but he cleared his throat again and avoided my eyes. "You have to admit it's a good line," he said.

I sank down in my chair and ran my hands through my hair. "This is fucking unreal."

"Are you going to call her?" he asked.

I stared at him yet again. "You think I should call her."

"I think you should do whatever makes you comfortable. Whatever makes you happy."

"This is why everyone hates therapists," I told him. "They talk in circles."

"Max, I'm here to help you through some serious trauma, not to give you advice on your love life." He paused. "But if you do date her, you should probably use condoms. Your doctor was right about that."

"I should never have told you that shit," I said.

"You should certainly tell me that shit," he countered. "You should tell me everything. That's how this works."

I leaned forward, put my elbows on my knees, and

pressed my hands to my eyes.

"How do you feel right now?" Dr. Weldman asked me. "Describe it."

I closed my eyes and looked for the words. I had to— he'd bug me until I did it. "I feel choked up," I said. "My chest hurts. My leg hurts. I feel fucking embarrassed, and mad at myself that I'm embarrassed. I can still smell her body lotion. I want to know what she thinks. I want to sit in my apartment and make the whole world go away. And I hate everyone."

"Everyone?"

"Absolutely fucking everyone."

"You used to only hate yourself," Dr. Weldman said. "I'm going to call that progress."

Chapter 7

Gwen

T HE OFFICES OF CANDY CANE, INCORPORATED WERE just off the elevator in an old office building that smelled vaguely of baked beans. Half the other tenants were moved out or out of business. Candy Cane was just a receptionist's desk and a single office behind it, containing the desk and telephone of Candy Cane's owner and president, Trent Wallace. Trent was a smarmy thirty-five-year-old with dyed black hair and a face you immediately wanted to punch. I figured he'd started a stripper business just to get close to the girls, but I'd never asked him, since that would mean actually talking to him when I didn't have to.

I had to talk to him today, unfortunately, because today was business. I brushed past the receptionist, who barely glanced up, since I was obviously one of the girls. Trent always gave instructions that "his girls" could come into his office, anytime.

He was sitting at his desk, typing away at his expensive computer—or pretending to type, who knew? I had no idea what Trent did all day, besides book us and take money. Maybe he spent the rest of his time on internet chat boards. It wouldn't surprise me.

"Gwen," he said, giving me a grin and sitting back.

I dropped into the office's only chair and crossed my legs. I was wearing jeans and a Wonder Woman t-shirt, just a little too tight. I was in the mood for guys to have to see Wonder Woman when they stared at my tits. That should have been his first warning.

"I want to talk to you," I said.

He kept grinning, obviously not getting my danger signals. "Sure. Anytime."

"I just got my paycheck. It's short—again."

"Is that so?" He didn't even try to look surprised, and I felt a spark of anger in my gut.

"The last three were short, too," I said. "And when I called, the receptionist said it was a mistake that would be made up on the next check. And yet every check gets shorter and shorter."

"How do you know it's short?" he asked. "Since you didn't even show up to that birthday gig this week, maybe you were docked for it."

I glared at him. Shit. "I was given the wrong apartment number," I said. "You can look it up. The system had the number wrong."

"And when you learned it was wrong, what did you do?" Trent asked. "Did you call in and ask what the right number was? No, you didn't. As far as I can tell, you just turned around and went home. You don't dance, you don't get paid. Those are the rules, Gwen."

I hadn't gone home, of course. I'd fucked the wrong

man instead, something I'd never done before. And even though it had been wild, dirty, practically anonymous sex, the thought of Trent, with his smarmy punchable face, finding out about it made me ill. "That doesn't explain the other checks," I said, deflecting him and staying on topic. "You're shorting me, Trent. Admit it."

He sighed. "I've instituted a practice of payment deferral. It's for the girls' own good."

I stared at him. "Payment deferral?"

"Yes. Part of every girl's paycheck is kept back. It's done on a sliding scale, so the girls who are in the most demand, and make the most, have the most held back." He smiled at me. "Think of it as a savings plan. Completely free."

"You have got to be fucking kidding me," I said. "You're keeping back the money I earned? You can't do that. It's illegal."

He shook his head. "It's in the employment contract you signed."

"Like hell it is." This was getting worse and worse. What the hell was going on?

"But it is," he argued. "There's a clause in the contract you signed when you started, stating that changes to the payment structure are at management's discretion. And management is me."

This was not happening. I was so angry I was practically seeing red, and at the same time a shiver of fear was working its way through my gut and up my spine. I owed back rent right now, and the check I'd received wasn't enough to cover it. "I never agreed for you to keep my money," I said. "Under this stupid setup of yours, when do I get the money I'm owed?"

"That's also at my discretion," Trent said smoothly. "However, in your case, I think maybe we can work something out."

I didn't like the sound of that. Not at all. "What are you talking about?"

"I have an exclusive party coming up on the schedule. Private, you know." He studied his fingernails, dropping his gaze for the first time. "I'm throwing it myself, and I need girls. There will be important people there that I need to impress. It's an opportunity for you, Gwen. If you do well, we can discuss releasing your back pay to you, plus a bonus."

"Wait a minute." I had to take a second to translate his self-serving words. "You're saying you want me to work one of your own parties, and do a private show?" I glared at him. "And what else am I supposed to do at this party?"

He kept his gaze on his fingernails and shrugged. "Who knows? There will be opportunities for you to make very good money. Let's just leave it at that."

Sex. He was talking about sex. My stomach churned. "No," I said. "That won't happen. We have a very simple deal, Trent. I show up, I do a show. A *show*. Then I collect my money and go home. I never agreed to a change in the deal. I want my back pay, and I'm not doing any party in order to get it."

He finally looked up again, and his face was hard, his eyes emotionless. He shrugged. "Then get a lawyer," he said.

I couldn't afford a lawyer on the pay I was getting, and he knew it. "And if I quit?"

"Then you forfeit the pay you're owed."

Which meant my rent didn't get paid, and I had no other skills, no other job. "So what do you suggest I do?"

"You either do the party, or you pick up extra assign-ments to make up the money. I'm sure Roberta at reception has some assignments you can take."

This wasn't easy, because most of the assignments were in the evening, and it wasn't possible to do more than two per night. There were the odd daytime gigs—the birthday one where I'd met Max was an example—but they were few and far between, usually office retirement parties, and any party that's at work, during the day, had terrible tips.

Trent knew all of this, of course. He was screwing me over so I'd do his party.

"Fuck you," I said, standing up. I needed to get out of here, rethink what the hell he'd just done to me and what I could do about it. "This isn't over."

"Don't be late for the softball team you have at five," he called after me as I walked out the door.

Outside, I got into my car and sat there, not turning the key, not moving, just staring out the windshield. I felt like throwing up.

I could get another job. The Bay area wasn't short of strip clubs. I could likely go in to any one of them and pick up some shifts, but that meant dancing on a pole every night in front of a drunk, rowdy audience. It wasn't much different than what I was doing now, and yet it was. In this job, I set my own pace, made my own hours, only worked late when I felt like it. I was independent, my own woman, doing what I wanted.

Or maybe I'd just been telling myself that.

I was twenty-six years old, and the only thing I knew how to do was get naked.

I scrubbed a hand over my face. I felt like someone was

sticking me with needles—I'd already had insomnia for two nights. Maybe I was going to have to do Trent's party. Maybe I could do it without being expected to have sex. And crazily, when I thought of that, I thought of Max Reilly—like I'd thought of him a thousand times since that day at his apartment.

I couldn't stop seeing his leg in my mind's eye. Couldn't stop. Not because it was ugly, or horrifying, but because it was just so—*final*. His leg was there, and then it just wasn't, and there was something else instead, the scars twisting over his skin. What had it taken for him to show that to me? What had it cost him? What the hell was I supposed to do with it?

An IED, he'd said. I knew what that was—Improvised Explosive Device. I'd made the mistake of Googling it. The results had left me shocked, sickened, robbed me of sleep. It was a bomb. A fucking *bomb*. And it had gone off so close it had taken part of his body. Burned it, exploded it.

I'd been shaken just Googling it, but he'd *lived* it. Was still living it.

A case of PTSD that nearly killed me.

I knew what that meant. I knew what he was implying. But I was too terrified to look at it too closely, wasn't I? Too chicken to think about it too deep. I kept everything on the surface, let nothing get too personal. While people like Max went and did things, experienced things, because they had no choice.

And my biggest problem was that my boss expected sex for money.

I stared at my phone. Max hadn't called me. Did he think I was an idiot? Was that why? Or was I supposed to call him? Would he take it the wrong way somehow, like pity? It wasn't pity. My hormones didn't care about his leg—I still wanted to jump him. Was that weird? Would he think it was weird?

As I sat there, thinking and stewing, my phone actually rang. I jumped, but it was my sister, Olivia. I tried to relax my jaw, my neck, which was a way to get the tension out of your voice. "Hey, sis," I said.

"Hey," she said. "You okay?"

Her sister ESP was in good shape. "Fine. Just, you know, had to talk to Trent."

"Ew. Did you disinfect?"

"On it."

"Good. What are you doing on Friday night?"

I tried not to breathe in relief. I couldn't talk about the thing with Trent right now. Olivia was supportive, but I knew she hated the fact that I worked as a stripper, and my mother agreed. They both wished I'd quit a long time ago, or never taken the job at all, and I'd always scoffed at their worries. It was humiliating to have to admit they were right.

As for the invitation, I used to go for drinks with my sister, but not since she'd fallen for Devon Wilder, Mr. Ridiculously Hot Billionaire, and moved in to his place in Diablo. "I'm not doing anything Friday night. What's up?"

"Devon and I want to take you to the theater."

I blinked. "A play?"

"*Macbeth,*" she said. "There's a big production on downtown. Devon is getting a box."

"He is?" I called up my mental picture of Devon Wilder. I'd met him a couple of times. He had been a criminal before spending two years in prison and inheriting from his unknown grandfather while he was inside. Even now, as suddenly rich as he was, he tended to wear jeans and t-shirts, and he had a tattoo on the back of his hand that said *No Time.* "I didn't know Devon was, um, a theater guy."

"He isn't," my sister said cheerfully, "but he's willing to try. We wanted to do something fun. And we wanted you to come."

I got it now. Of the two of us, I was the performer while Olivia was the shy one. I'd spent a year in acting school before dropping out. I'd never seriously pursued being an actress, but Olivia knew it was something I was interested in, and she was trying to come up with something I'd like to do.

In short, this was about me. Or, more likely, about me and Devon. Olivia wanted us to be friends. Not that we weren't. We were strangers, sort of. I was wary of him, because he had the power to utterly break my sister's heart, and there was nothing I could do about it. He seemed equally wary of me, probably because I had been the closest person in Olivia's life before he came along.

I sighed. "Liv, you don't have to do this."

"What? I'm not doing anything. It'll be fun."

"Setting me up with Devon. We'll be fine. I mean, he can beat me up, so what am I gonna do?"

"Gwen, he offered to sit in a theater box. For three hours. For you."

No, I almost corrected her, *for you.* I pinched the bridge of my nose. I shouldn't argue this. Olivia was happy—amazingly happy. She was my sister, and we were close. If she wanted me to go to *Macbeth* and be a third wheel while reminding myself how single and miserable I was, I could do it.

Besides, the production would probably be really good.

"Okay," I said, thinking of my pathetic paycheck. "As long as he's paying."

Olivia laughed. "He's paying."

"And I want—" I tried to think of something that would make it a little less easy on him. "I want a limo to pick me up."

"Done."

"And I want him to take me to hotwire cars, or whatever it is that ex-cons do, some other time so he doesn't think he has to do this crap all the time to impress me."

She was laughing again, a truly happy sound that made my stomach twist. "Okay, okay, hotwire cars or something. Got it."

"Friday night, then."

I hung up and sat in the silence of my car again. I felt a little bit better, but not a lot. It was going to be a nice evening. But I was going to be alone.

I'd always preferred being alone. I'd dated, but I hadn't had any long-term relationships, any men who I'd been particularly committed to. It always went a certain way: Man pursued me; I said no; man kept pursuing; I finally relented with conditions; if man met certain conditions I dated him for a while, eventually including sex, until I was tired of him. Then I dumped him. Repeat.

That was the way I'd always preferred it. And I stared at the parking lot past my windshield and had the sudden, profound realization that, like the rest of my life, it was completely fucking awful. Twisted and lonely, painful and a little sick. I wanted to reach backward in my life and erase it, erase everything, scrub every bit of it out with bleach.

My phone rang again, and this time my chest went tight, my throat constricted. It was Max Reilly.

My voice came out breathless when I answered, though I hadn't intended it to. "Hey there," I said.

His voice was its usual cranky growl. "Gwen?"

"Yes, Max?"

He paused for a second, probably taken aback by how excited I sounded, and then he said, "Okay. I'm going for a beer later tonight. If you want to come."

My mouth dropped open. I forgot about my problems for a minute and remembered that he was completely fucking *adorable*. "Are you asking me on a date?" I asked sweetly.

"It's not a date," he said.

"Right. Because you don't want a blow job."

"*Jesus*. I—" He paused, and I let him hang. "Fuck. I'm going to be there, whether you want to come or not. That's what I'm saying. It's the place I usually go."

Now I was intrigued. I wanted to know every little thing about Max Reilly's life, starting with what bar he usually went to. "All right," I said. "Maybe I'll come." I twisted a lock of hair over my finger. "What should I wear?"

"*Clothes*, Gwen. For God's sake, wear clothes. Lots of them. There are guys there."

"Guys? Lawdy. What will I do?"

"You'll have a beer with me," he said, as if this were a serious question. And then he added, "If you want."

I just stared out the windshield of my parked car, thinking about how he managed to make me swoon with absolutely no intention to.

"Gwen?" He sounded worried, like he thought he'd pissed me off.

"Tell me where this bar is," I said, and when he answered I said, "I've never been to that neighborhood. I've never even heard of it."

"That's because it's a shit neighborhood," he replied. "So, yeah, wear clothes."

"A beer with Max Reilly, who doesn't want a date, in a shit neighborhood," I said. "What girl could say no?"

He paused. "Shit," he said. "I suck at this, don't I?"

I checked the time. "I'll be there at seven," I said, and hung up.

That would show him.

He didn't have to know I was smiling.

Chapter 8

Max

I WASN'T LYING—EDISON'S BAR WAS IN A SHIT neighborhood, of which South San Francisco had plenty. Even though it had a view of the bay, it was on a crummy street lined with smoke shops and laundromats, overlooking a desolate concrete pier and the choppy, frigid water beyond. No tourist had ever come within a mile of this place.

Gwen wasn't there when I got there, but I was early. It was best if I got there first; I had no idea what the patrons of Edison's would do if they saw a woman like Gwen walk in alone. Probably quietly suffocate over their pints while trying to get up the nerve to talk to her, but you never knew.

I had on jeans, a black sweater to keep out the chill in the evening air, and black boots. I liked San Francisco's climate a lot better than LA's, because it was so much colder. When I had jeans and boots on, you couldn't spot my leg unless it was a bad day and I was limping. No way was I going back to a place where people wore shorts and sandals all the time. Some guys with legs like mine had no problem wearing shorts, but I wasn't one of them. I'd always looked like the coldest guy in the city.

I nodded at the bartender, Jason Edison—the son of the owner—and found a seat in a corner booth. There were a handful of guys here tonight, some of them sitting at the bar and watching the Giants game, some of them just sitting, drinking, staring at nothing. They nodded at me, I nodded at them—we were all regulars. One old guy read a paper newspaper through his half glasses, slowly turning the pages with a hand that was covered in old scars.

I ordered a pint and pulled out my phone so I would have something to look at while I waited. If I got stood up—which seemed likely, since my skills with women, especially Gwen, were nonexistent—at least no one would know. I came here at least once a week just to get out of my apartment and look at four different walls for a change. The other guys here understood me, and the owners didn't care that I never drank much.

She hadn't called or texted. There was an email from the construction company I worked for, asking if I would be available for some shifts next week. I stared at it, thinking it over.

It seemed like a no-brainer. Devon had given me five million dollars, and I didn't have to work again until I chose to. If I invested it, it could last me the rest of my life. But what the fuck would I do then? I wasn't a guy cut out for living a life of leisure. In the Marines, every minute of our day had been structured, even the minutes when you were sleeping or sitting around bored, waiting for something to happen. You always had somewhere you were supposed to be.

And then I'd been hurt, and there had been a long period with rounds of surgeries and recoveries. I'd worked as much as I could through the Bad Time, when I'd been doing physical and mental therapy, because I had my father's debts to pay on top of my own. I'd worked every minute I was upright, taking any job that would have me, trying to pay my way.

And now I didn't have to do that. I didn't have to work construction with half a leg and lie awake every night worrying about money. Dad was dead, Devon had give me money, and my whole life had changed. It was incredible—Devon was incredible. My heart sped up, my blood pounding in my ears. I felt sweat between my shoulder blades, clammy and cold.

As I did sometimes when I had these attacks, I pictured Dr. Weldman, heard his voice in my head. *What are you feeling right now? Describe it.*

Fear, I told him. *I'm feeling fear.*

Here is the thing about PTSD: it's the fear your brain has been trained to feel, and you can't turn it off. In combat, you're always ready; you see a possible threat in every direction. When you get home, your brain keeps it up. You can't just leave it behind, snap out of it, because your brain has the signal that *you're about to fucking die.* Even when you're standing in line at the bank or trying to remember where you parked your car. Four years of treatment had made me better than I used to be, but it could still sneak up on me, bring me to my knees. I pictured my happy place, the path in the fall woods, while sweat broke out on me and my vision swam.

There was a whispered hush in the bar. I looked up and

saw Gwen walking toward me.

She was wearing jeans and beaded sandals. She had on a white top made of flowy material that was just snug enough over her incredible breasts before dropping modestly down. Her blond hair was loose and she had only a little makeup on. Every male in Edison's Bar looked poleaxed.

She sat down across from me in the booth. She had lip gloss on, and I had the sudden desire to taste it, lick every speck of it off her mouth. At the thought, I felt my panic spiral away like water down a drain. But it wasn't quite gone, so all I managed to say was, "If you didn't have to work anymore, would you?"

If my conversation opener surprised her, she didn't show it. She just blinked at me and gave me a glare with those dark-lashed, sexy blue eyes. "Max," she said, "Today I had to strip in front of a fucking softball team. What do you think my answer is?"

I felt myself frowning at her. In my fucked-up head, there'd been a moment when I'd forgotten she was a stripper. And suddenly, it bothered me. A fuck of a lot.

I leaned back in my seat and tried to get a grip. Gwen wasn't my business. It wasn't my business that guys saw her naked every day. I'd seen her naked, after all, because she was on one of her jobs. She wasn't fucking the guys—she'd said so, and I believed her. They were just looking. And even if she was fucking them, it was none of my goddamned business.

"You're scowling," she pointed out.

I had too much going around in my head. But one crazy thought floated to the surface: I had five million dollars. I could make it so that Gwen didn't have to take her clothes off to make a living anymore.

I barely knew her, but I already knew one thing: If I suggested that to her, she'd kick me in the balls.

"Sorry," I said, hedging and trying to erase the no doubt terrifying frown from my expression. "I was just thinking."

She raised her eyebrows, waiting for me to go on, then prompted me. "About what?"

"Quitting my job." I looked down at my phone, and realized I already knew the answer. While she watched, I texted to my foreman that I wouldn't be available for any more shifts, ever again, and pressed send. "In fact, I just did."

She looked surprised, then turned and raised a hand to Jason behind the bar. Normally it took an act of God to get Jason's attention, but the minute Gwen turned her blond head, he darted from behind the bar, came to our booth, and took her drink order. When he was gone, she turned back to me, completely unaware she'd upset the natural order of things with one painted fingernail. "Continue," she commanded. "What is—was—your job?"

"Construction." There was only a flicker of expression on her face, but I was attuned to it, so I picked it up. "Stop," I told her. "I can do the work with half a leg. I've been doing it for years."

She had the grace not to deny it; she just shrugged. "Okay. But you just quit? How do you afford that?"

Shit. I wasn't going to tell her I had five million dollars. She barely knew me, and she'd just walked in. I'd sound like an asshole trying to impress her with money, instead of just the general asshole she already thought I was. "It's just a thought I had," I said. "I can afford to take some time off."

Gwen narrowed her eyes at me, not even glancing at

Jason as he put her beer in front of her. He wandered off, disappointed. "You are very mysterious, you know that?" She sipped her beer and looked around. "What is this place, anyway? It's like a literal man cave."

"I guess it is," I said. It was true, I'd never once seen a woman in Edison's. "It's what I'm used to, I suppose," I explained. "You should see the gym I go to. It's basically some guy's sweat sock."

"I think your whole life is a sweat sock," she countered, sipping her beer again. "You give off this sort of… testosterone-smell. Do you interact with any real, live women? At all?"

I pretended to think it over. "The woman behind the counter at the gas station looked at me today," I said. "Does that count?"

She tutted in response, looking me over. "Such a waste."

I went still as a pulse of attraction arced between us, my breath going short. The panic had gone, and now I remembered what it had looked like when I'd unzipped her dress, when she'd rubbed herself on my lap, nearly getting herself off. *Do it,* she'd said to me, and *Harder.* As if she was reading my mind, her tongue darted out and licked her glossy bottom lip.

"To answer your question," I said, clearing my throat, "the guy who owns this place is a veteran. So is his son, who's the guy behind the bar. It's mostly vets in here. That's why I come."

Now it was Gwen's turn to frown. "So a bunch of guys with something in common come here to sit alone and not talk to each other. Do I have that right?"

"You don't know very many veterans, do you?" I said.

"We don't talk about anything. Ever. Especially important shit. A night of not talking is our idea of bliss."

"Fine." She leaned forward, across the table toward me, lowering her voice, oblivious to what the pose did to her incredible tits inside her shirt. "As long as none of them drop their pants for me." She gave me half a smile. "Again."

I took a sip of beer. "I didn't drop 'em all the way the first time."

She blinked, and her pupils went dark as she remembered the two of us on my sofa, my cock inside her, just like I did. The moment stretched out, the air between us so thick I could have put out my tongue and tasted it. And in that second, I forgot everything that was wrong. I just *was*, a guy with a beer and a crazy sexy woman and a half-hard dick in his jeans, on the edge of something that excited me and didn't scare me in the least.

Her gaze traveled down my throat, my shoulders, my chest, and back up again. "I like you," she said, still leaning forward, her voice practically a whisper. "We should have some more sex."

I sent a pointed look down to her chest in return, then raised my eyes to hers again. "There's a pool table in the back." I watched her eyes go wide, and then I said, "You want to play some pool?"

"Naughty," she said, but her eyes flashed, and I learned something: This woman was competitive. "You know I'm going to beat you, right?"

My pool skills were average, but I wasn't about to tell her that. "You can try."

"Okay, beard man," she said, sliding out of her seat. "You're on."

Chapter 9

Gwen

H E WAS DRIVING ME CRAZY. EVERY TIME I WON AT pool, he'd win the next game, so we were neck and neck. I did not do well with neck and neck. I did well with winning.

"You're doing this on purpose," I said to him after our sixth game, when we were three and three.

"I'm not," he argued. "I'm trying to win."

"Well, try harder," I told him. "Or less hard."

He gave me a look at that, and we went back to playing again.

A few of the guys in the bar drifted in and out of the room, watching us. They didn't say much; they seemed happy to just be spectators. I was used to being watched by men, but this was different, and it took me some time to realize why. They were looking at me, which was fine, but none of them were leering. Because they all assumed that I was with Max. That we were a couple.

And maybe they were watching me, but I wanted to watch *him*. Max Reilly had a presence, a way of moving, that I'd never seen in any other man. He wasn't quick, or lithe, but he was powerful. Strong. His walk was distinctive, slightly off-kilter, though he wasn't limping like he'd been the day I'd met him in front of his door. He didn't move a lot, just like he didn't talk a lot. When it was time for me to take my shot, he just leaned his hip against the high-top table in the corner, his fingers idly drumming on his pool cue, and waited.

That dark hair. That dark beard, cut close to his jaw but a little scruffy. He had high cheekbones under there, and a nice mouth that had kissed me just the way I liked it. His intelligent eyes watched me steadily, but gave nothing away.

And I was slowly going nuts. I was jumpy in my skin, skittish, painfully horny. I wanted his hands on me, but he wouldn't do it. I wanted to fuck him, but I didn't know exactly how to get him to agree. Should I be seductive? Flirtatious? Direct? Or should I back off and wait?

Is this what it's normally like for guys? I wondered to myself as I watched him circle the table, looking for his shot. *I think I understand them better now.*

And for that hour, I forgot about everything. I forgot about Trent and my money problem and my back rent and the images I'd seen when I'd Googled *IED*. I forgot that he wasn't my type and there was no way we belonged together, even for a game of pool. I just watched him and looked for signals, like any ordinary woman on a date would do.

He bent to take a shot and I leaned over his shoulder, trying the direct approach. "Gutter it, and I'll sleep with you."

He glanced at me, his brow furrowed, then looked back at the table. "Nope."

And he sunk it, the bastard.

I had a second beer, but Max only had one. When he won the seventh game, breaking our tie, I took the last swig of my beer and put down my cue. "Fine," I said.

Max watched me, his body suddenly still. "We done?" he asked.

I shrugged. "I admit defeat."

"Thank fucking God." He put his own cue down and grabbed my wrist. "Let's go."

Well, damn—it looked like I'd already won. I tried not to laugh in triumph as he led me out the door.

* * *

We went back to his apartment, which was what I wanted. My place was nicer, but it was tiny, and somehow Max didn't belong there. Besides, against all odds I *liked* Shady Oaks, with its cracked concrete, empty pool filled with leaves and old beer bottles, and undeniably criminal neighbors. I liked Max's place, full of his personality, his well-read books and his t-shirt tossed over the back of the sofa. I didn't want to be girly tonight. I wanted to be buried in him, surrounded by him, wrapped in is delicious smell. In his bed.

He followed me into the apartment and I kicked off my sandals. I'd been uncertain when we were in the bar, but now that we were in his place, I thought my chances were good. I was pretty certain. I had to remember that the way Max was, he would likely never make a move in a public place.

But in private…

I walked into his kitchen, not even glancing at him, every inch of my skin alive with anticipation. "You got anything to drink?" I asked. "I think I'd like—"

He spun me around, pinned me against the counter, and kissed me.

I opened my mouth immediately and bit him. He bit me back, kissing me harder, scraping my skin. He put his hands on my jaw and pressed into me, and I slid my arms around his waist, feeling the heat and hardness of his chest against me, his stomach, his back beneath my hands. We'd never kissed standing up before, and our bodies fit perfectly, even though he was taller than me, more muscled. If he broke the kiss, I'd be able to fit the curve of my cheek right on to the taut, warm skin of his neck. If I sank to my knees, I'd be the perfect height to suck him off.

He dropped his mouth to the soft skin beneath my ear, kissed roughly down my neck, and paused. "Fuck," he said, his breath warm on my skin.

I moved my hands back around his front and pushed up his black sweater and the t-shirt underneath. I slid my palms over his taut, perfect stomach, slowly scratched my nails through the line of hair beneath his belly button. "You nervous?" I asked him. "We've already done this."

But I was lying, and we both knew it. We hadn't done this, not exactly. We'd fucked, and that seemed like a lot, but it wasn't everything. It was far from everything.

Right now, I wanted everything. Everything I could get.

He lifted his head and kissed me again, slower this time, sliding his tongue along the inside of my lower lip, exploring me as he cradled my head. He was still pinning me to the counter, and I could feel his heat through his clothes, feel the tantalizing shape and hardness of his cock in his jeans. I was already wet. I groaned softly into his mouth.

He pulled away, and something flashed across his expression, something that looked a little like alarm. "I should…" He looked away from me, frowned to himself. "Wait a second."

He left me, and I heard him walk to the sofa, sit down. I turned to see him bent down, taking off his boots.

He'd gone back inside his head. I'd watched it. It had something to do with his leg, with feeling awkward about it. He wanted his boots off to have sex. Did he not want me to see his leg? He'd already showed it to me, by his own choice, without my asking. I didn't know, but I sensed the change, back to lost-in-thought Max, and it wasn't what I wanted. I wanted passionate, turned-on, dirty-kissing Max back.

So I followed him to the sofa and stood in front of him. He glanced up at me just as I pulled my shirt off over my head and dropped it, leaving only my lacy bra.

The breath hushed out of him, and his eyes went wide. "Wait," he said.

"No way." I stepped forward, between his knees, pushing his apart with mine. For a second I felt the familiarity—him on the sofa, me standing in front of him, taking my clothes off—but I felt the difference, too. The hushed quiet, the lack of a show. I knew exactly what I wanted. I watched his face as I dropped to my knees between his legs.

He knew what I was doing, and he looked turned on and almost panicked at the same time. "Gwen."

"Be quiet." I put my palms on his thighs—oh, I liked his thighs. Thick with muscle, hard and warm. I slid my hands up and began to unbuckle his belt.

He went still, his body tight, his muscles tense. Wanting it, and feeling some kind of instinct to stop it. I opened his belt, the top button on his jeans, the next button. He didn't stop it.

I was turned on. I wanted this; it was the only thing on my mind. And he had no idea, but this wasn't my usual method at all. When a guy got sex with me—which wasn't a given—we started out with the usual: intercourse, me on my back. If he passed that test, I might get creative, but only if I was feeling generous. A blow job was for much further down the line—weeks, maybe. I'd never given a man a blow job without making him beg for it.

But I slid my hand inside Max's boxers, and he made a little sound, and I just wanted his cock. I *wanted* it. I'd felt it, what it could do, but I wanted to see it up close. Taste it. As I pushed down his jeans and boxers, he flexed his hips as it came free, and I curled my fingers around it, palming it and feeling every contour.

His voice was choked, strangled as he watched me. "I thought you were joking about the blow job."

"I wasn't," I said, and bent and took him in my mouth.

He tensed again, almost like it hurt. Did he not do this very much? I didn't know. I slid up and down him experimentally, using my tongue, trying to get him to relax. He just choked another breath, his thighs hard as granite against me.

But he didn't stop me, and I leaned into it, getting my rhythm, making him feel it. He tasted good, and I used my tongue more than I usually did, savoring the texture and flavor of his skin. I tilted my head just right so my hair fell forward, and I knew he was looking at my blonde hair trailing over his sweater, which was still pulled over his stomach, my bare shoulders beyond.

I went slow, savoring not only the taste of him, but the power. He was already close. I had done that. I had this big, perfect man under my control, and for once it wasn't a game—it was a gift. One he gave me, and one I gave him. He was trusting me, letting me feel his raw reaction, letting me lead. And it was, without a doubt, the sexiest, most erotic thing I'd ever done, even after all the times I'd taken my clothes off.

I took him deeper, pressing down more boldly, inhaling him, feeling his cock in the back of my throat. His big body flinched again in the intensity of the pleasure, and I felt him flex in my mouth, close to coming. The pulse between my legs beat heavy and hard. I wanted that, to taste his come, but I wanted everything else, too.

As if he'd read my mind, I felt his hand on the side of my head, the gentle pressure of his fingers. I let him go and looked up at him. His eyes were impossibly dark in the half light of the apartment, and in the shadows his lashes looked long, his face harsh and beautiful. He was breathing hard.

"Get in my bed," he said.

Yes, sir. I licked my lips and stood, walking through the doorway that had to be his bedroom. I was right. It was like the rest of his apartment, tidy but masculine, the bed made but the pillows rumpled, a pair of jeans crumpled on the floor, laundry flowing out of a basket, a dog-eared book next to the dark bedside lamp. A window held light from an electric light in the corridor, covered by a simple blind.

I lay on my back on the bed, feeling the cool blanket beneath me. Max followed me into the room, pulling his shirt and sweater off in one motion.

I was reaching for the button on my jeans, but I paused.

I hadn't seen him shirtless yet—another first, another thing we hadn't done yet. He was powerful, his chest and stomach lightly dusted with dark hair, his hips lithe, with indents disappearing into his undone jeans. I saw the tattoo I'd glimpsed the first day we met, something that criss-crossed his left shoulder and down onto his glorious bicep. He ran a hand through his hair, mussing it further, and looked down at me.

It was the same look he'd given me that first time on his sofa, the one that said he wanted to fuck me but was keeping himself in check. Holding his gaze, I undid my jeans button and zipper, lifting my hips off the bed and hooking my fingers in the waistband. When I slid the jeans down I did a sinuous little wiggle with my hips—just a small one, and then another, a quick stripper shimmy.

No man I dated, ever, got a strip show from me. Any man who thought that dating a stripper meant he would get free dances all the time didn't get past my initial test. I said it was because I did the shows for money, not for free, but the real reason was that I didn't want a man who only wanted a performer, not a woman. A man who wanted a performer instead of me.

But Max... Max already wanted me. And I gave him the shimmy, the hip twist, without thinking. He liked it, but it wasn't the only thing he wanted from me. He didn't want a show.

He approached the bed as I kicked my jeans off. Without ceremony he pulled off my panties—thin, white, plain cotton—and tossed them away. Then he parted my legs and got on the bed between them.

I relaxed, letting him look, wondering what was next.

My blood was going haywire, my skin oversensitive to the touch. I unhooked my bra and tossed it away. I felt the warmth of his breath, because I was waxed bare—an occupational requirement. He'd seen it before, but this time he took it in, his head between my legs, looking at my pussy, and I wished I could see his expression better, gage his reaction.

He lifted a hand and ran a thumb over my wet seam. "I can see how wet you are for me," he growled.

"I am," I said, my voice a breath. "Fuck, I am."

He slid the thumb deeper into me, sliding it through my wetness, and then he parted me. There was no hiding how swollen and soaked I was, how easily his fingers slid over me. He explored me softly with his fingertips, making me squirm, and then he made soft circles around my clit, tighter and tighter. "Max," I said. Pleading, maybe.

He stopped the circling and lowered his hand. "I'm gonna taste," he said, and then he lowered his mouth to me.

I cried out and pulsed my hips up, practically grinding into his mouth, his beard. It was so wildly hot, his mouth on me. He slid his tongue over me, and I could have come, but he cut it short. He lifted his mouth off me and replaced it with his fingers again, sliding over me, edging inside me.

He crawled up my body, his hand still between my legs. His chest brushed my nipples, sending electric shocks through me. His jeans were still halfway down his legs where I'd shoved them down, not all the way off. But he pressed down on top of me, his fingers still between us, and he kissed me, open and dirty, letting me taste myself, taste me and him mixed together.

When he broke the kiss, he removed his hand, bracing

it on the mattress. "You want it?" he said, his breath feathering my mouth. "You want my cock?"

"Yes," I said. I was nearly begging now, I wanted it so bad. "Yes."

His big hand gripped my knee and he slid his cock over me, letting it feel my wetness. "You like it," he said. "My cock."

Damn, I guess he'd observed that. Well, I hadn't been subtle. "I do," I said, and I leaned up and licked his bottom lip, my tongue running over the rough edge of his beard. "You have a sweet cock, Max Reilly."

His arms flexed, and in a twist of his hips he thrust inside me, filling me.

I groaned. He pumped me, slow and rhythmic, seeming to know exactly what I needed. *You're a woman who wanted to get fucked,* he'd said before. I was. I pressed my legs as wide as I could, took him as deep as I could. I wanted to feel him so deep it hurt.

He kept his pace, but he dropped his face to my neck and reached one big arm up, gripping the headboard. "Fuck me," he said in my ear. "Take me deep and fuck me."

Then he slammed into me harder, picking up his pace. I could feel it in my whole body, my breasts shaking, my stomach slick against his. I cried out, reaching my hands around to grip his ass, which was hard and solid and perfect. He fucked me harder, finding that rhythm with my body that we'd found the first time, both of us in perfect sync.

The headboard was banging against the wall, and I was making all kinds of sounds. After a minute the neighbor next door banged on the wall, shouting for us to stop. But I didn't care. I wanted all of Shady Oaks to hear us. I wanted all of them to know that Max Reilly was fucking me, that he was giving it to me hard. That Max Reilly was going to make me come.

And he did. With just his cock, with his hips pounding into me and his hand braced on the headboard, his body pleasuring mine, he made me come. I shouted as I felt the orgasm blast through me, screamed his name, didn't hold back. "That's it," he said against my skin as he pounded me even harder, racing to come. "Fuck, that's it. That's right."

I bit his shoulder, gripped his ass, tilted my hips up to take him deeper. "Do it," I said, my own orgasm still rippling with aftershocks. "Oh, God, yes, come inside me, come inside me—"

He cried out, a sexy sound in his throat, and flexed inside me, hard. We stayed frozen for a long moment, connected, neither wanting to let go.

Finally he rolled off me, onto his back, panting. "Shit," he said. "That wasn't supposed to happen."

I breathed out a laugh. My body was in a state of bliss— my restlessness gone, my blood like warm honey in my veins. I couldn't think of a single problem in my life right now—not one. "I think we happen," I said, letting my eyes drift closed. "Get used to it."

I was boneless and relaxed, but I felt him sit up, wrestle with his jeans which were still on his legs. "I didn't even take my leg off," he grumbled.

"Do you usually?" I asked, curious and hoping it was okay. "Take your leg off for sex?"

He pulled off his jeans and dropped them to the floor. He took so long answering I decided it was a rude question, but then he said, "I'd rather, I guess."

It seemed an odd answer—either you took it off or you didn't. But I really, really didn't want to explore the idea of him fucking some other woman like he'd just fucked me, so I didn't pursue it. Instead I drifted with my eyes closed while I listened to him get up, go into the bathroom, run the water. He came back with a hot, wet cloth, and I dabbed between my legs while he sat on the edge of the bed, removing his leg. His big back was thick with muscle, the ridge of his spine flawless as he bent, and I could see the curve of his ass, which made my mouth water. I wanted him to get back over here. I wanted that big body between my legs again. I also wanted to sleep for a week.

"What are you looking at?" he asked without looking back at me.

"Your butt," I answered.

He shook his head, then glanced back over his shoulder at me. "Most people would stare at the leg."

"I can't see it from here. And I'm not most people."

"I'm getting that part." There was a thump as his leg hit the floor, and then he pulled the covers down and slid onto the bed, lying down. I could look at that body for years, centuries. He was hairier than any man I'd been with, though he wasn't particularly hairy, I supposed—he had some dark hair on his chest, some whorls in a line down the center of his stomach, and his cock was in a dark, glorious nest of pubic hair.

I made my eyes travel lower before I made a fool of myself. Jesus, he was just a man. There were millions of them out there. "Can I look at your leg?" I asked him.

"No." Not hostile, but definitive.

"I don't think it's weird," I said. "I want to see it."

"Nope. Go away."

I huffed a breath and pulled the covers down on my side, climbing under them. "I'm not leaving, by the way," I told him. "I'm staying. You're stuck with me in your bed."

His chest rose and fell, and I pressed next to him, feeling his muscles relax as he stared at the ceiling. He was warm as a furnace. I again had the desire both to sleep and to fuck him raw at the same time. "My bed's going to smell like coconut," he observed.

"It's my body lotion." I sidled even closer, letting my cheek rest against his shoulder. His bachelor's bed, in this crummy apartment building, was somehow nicer than mine. "You smell nice," I said, which was an understatement, because his warmth and his smell were making my whole body feel good. "Not like a sweat sock."

He might have said something in reply. I didn't know. I was already asleep.

Chapter 10

Max

THERE WAS A WOMAN IN MY BED. A REAL ONE.

She was hot, and sexy, and wild, and that made me uncomfortable enough. But I kept circling back to the fact that there was an actual woman in my bed, like it was amazing. Because it *was* amazing.

Before Gwen, the last woman I'd had sex with was the girlfriend I'd had while I was deployed. We'd slept together on my last leave, which I remembered, because we'd broken up soon afterward. I'd gone back to Afghanistan, and three months later an IED had ended my career.

I hadn't had sex since before I lost my leg. Four years. Until Gwen showed up at my apartment.

She'd been so casual, asking if I usually had sex with my leg on. She had no idea it was a situation that had never come up.

I didn't feel the need to enlighten her. She'd probably think I was even stranger than she already did.

She was still asleep, though the sun was coming up behind the blinds in my window. Asleep, she was just as beautiful as ever, her features relaxed, her hair tousled, her skin pearly and smooth. She'd slept heavily all night, barely moving. I had been more restless, my body pleasantly tired after the sex—Jesus, that had been incredible—but my brain doing its usual ticking over. I was used to it—sleep was both my friend and my enemy.

At least I hadn't had any nightmares last night. But I found myself wishing I could just sleep for once instead of thinking too much.

This was a one-time thing. She's going to leave in the morning. It's going to be awkward.

This isn't a one-time thing. She's going to want to see you again. What are you going to say?

You see? My fucked-up brain.

I sat up in bed, rummaged on the floor for my leg, and put it on. Part of me didn't want her to see me like this; it was too exposed for me, too intimate. No one had seen my body up close in four years except doctors, and that was the way I liked it. No one to see, really see, what it looked like. It was easier that way. I could do that this morning, too. Just put jeans on before she woke up and avoid the whole thing.

Instead, I put on a clean pair of boxers and walked out into the kitchen to make coffee.

I had put it all in the maker and was watching it drip when I heard her get up, shuffle around the bedroom, go into the bathroom. Oh, fuck. I stared at the ceiling. Was my bathroom a mess? Shit, I couldn't remember.

I heard her come out, into the kitchen behind me. I kept my back turned.

"Hey," she said.

Don't be an asshole, Max. Turn around.

I did.

She was wearing my shirt.

My stomach dropped and did a strange twist. It was the shirt I'd worn under my sweater last night, that I'd dropped on the floor. She had it on now—and, it looked like, nothing else. The hem of the shirt went to the middle of her thighs.

She ran a hand through her tousled blonde hair, her eyes on me, and I saw a flicker of uncertainty there, like she wasn't sure what I would think.

I cleared my throat. "You want some coffee?" I asked.

She shrugged, dropped her hand again. I turned back to the coffee. Fuck. I should say something. I *wanted* to say something, but my words wouldn't come. They never came when it was important, and sometimes they didn't come at all. This was my fucking problem.

She came around the counter and stood next to me. The uncertain look was gone, or maybe buried, and she gave me a sweetly flirtatious look instead. "You're cute when you're tongue-tied," she said.

I banged a mug on the counter. "I'm not cute," I grumbled. "You want sugar?"

"Can I ask you something?"

"Probably not."

"What's your tattoo?" She reached up a hand and traced the ink on my shoulder, down my bicep.

My body roared to life when she touched me, but I kept it locked down. I took my hand off the coffee cup and looked down at my shoulder, watching her pretty, manicured fingertip tracing it. "It's initials," I said.

"I can see the letters here," she said, looking closely in the daylight, sliding her fingertip over the swirls of the stylized initials. "What do they mean?"

"J, D, K," I said, quoting the letters. "James, David, Keishon. They died in the attack."

"Oh," she said softly, with an edge of sadness, tracing the letters again. She didn't have to ask what attack.

"I lived," I said. "They died. It seemed the least I could do."

"It's nice," she said. Her fingertip left my shoulder and moved along my collarbone. "If that was my brother, I'd be glad you did it."

"You have a brother?"

"No." She didn't elaborate, just traced her hand along my collarbone and down my chest. She seemed to be looking closely at me in the daylight, which was exactly what I'd been dreading—and yet now that she was doing it, I didn't mind. I looked at her face while her eyes were lowered. Even in the tired light of the morning after, with her hair messy and her makeup long gone, she was unfuckingbelievable. I had no idea why this woman was in my kitchen, wearing nothing but my shirt.

"We really have nothing in common, do we?" she asked, letting her touch slide down my chest to my stomach. "I mean, you have all of those terrible experiences overseas, and I dropped out of acting school and became a stripper."

I winced. I didn't like to think of her job, not right now. Not when she was looking at me like no other woman ever had. "We have plenty in common," I replied, my voice gruff. "We both like sex."

That made her smile in just the right way—amused and a little wicked. She raised her eyes back to mine, though she kept her hand on my bare stomach, tousling the hair there.

"No way, Max," she said, her voice teasing. "I know a bachelor pad when I see one. You don't have any women here."

When you put it that way, it was painfully obvious.
"Maybe I go to hotels," I said. "I'm a hotel guy."

She shook her head, smiling now.

"I kick them out the next morning," I tried. "A new one
every day."

"Nope." She inched her hand down toward the waist of
my boxers, and I made myself breathe.

"Okay," I said. "I don't do it very often." *Like, not at all in
four years.* "Unlike you, who gets laid every time she snaps
her fingers, no doubt."

She blinked at me, and her expression went serious. "I
have sex," she said, unaware she was giving me a twist in my
gut, "but that doesn't mean I like it."

I was so surprised at this that I laughed. "You could
have fooled me. My neighbors heard everything. They think
I'm Zeus right now."

"Yeah, well, you kind of are," she said with that same serious expression. "Last night was different. It wasn't…" She
trailed off, and I watched her put her thoughts together. "It
wasn't a negotiation."

I had no idea what that meant. I should probably know.
I should probably be understanding here, say something
wise. I had the feeling she was talking about something she
didn't normally talk about. But as usual, I didn't have anything perfect to say, and I was quiet so long that she looked
up at me with a worried frown. "What?" she said.

"I don't get it," I told her. "The negotiation thing. I mean,
fuck me or don't fuck me. It's up to you."

She blinked up at me, and slowly her features relaxed,

a smile touching the corners of her mouth. Suddenly I was aware that she still had her hand on my stomach, and that awareness shot straight downward. She let her eyes drop down to my shoulders, my arms, my chest, and her tongue briefly touched the edge of her upper lip, the sight making me start to get hard. "I see," she said, her voice soft.

It was a game, but it wasn't. She was flirting, but she wasn't. Underneath it she was looking at me like she wanted to devour me, like she was very fucking turned on. And suddenly I wondered if she was wet—if I touched that bare, sexy pussy like I had last night, if my fingers would slide over it, slide into her slick and deep with no resistance.

And I knew she wanted me to.

I put my hands under the hem of her shirt—my shirt—and moved them up her body, cupping her breasts beneath the fabric. I ran my thumbs over her nipples slowly, taking my time. She had incredible breasts, big enough to fill my hands to overflowing, soft and warm and firm. She stood still as I touched them. Her breath stopped. Her pupils went dark. Her nipples went hard.

I looked at her, saw her watching me, my face. "You want more?" I asked her.

"Yes," she breathed, her eyes never leaving me.

I stepped closer, brushed my mouth over hers. "You're insatiable."

"You should talk." The hand on my stomach moved, tugged down my boxer shorts, and curled around my cock, which was hard as iron now. She stroked it, her soft skin working me all the way down to my balls, then back up again.

I made some kind of angry sound and pressed her back

so she was against the counter again, like she'd been last night. But this time I kept her there, biting her neck gently as she stroked me again and again, as my body went wild. If we kept this up I was going to come, probably sooner than I wanted—I'd never had a woman's touch that felt like hers. So I said, "Tell me what you want."

"Make me come," she breathed.

I gripped her hips and lifted her onto the counter, sucking the soft place beneath her jaw. "Open your legs and I'll do it."

"Fuck," she said, one dirty little murmur, and then she opened her knees and hooked them around my hips as I braced myself on the counter. She was bare and wet, and I slid my cock over her, savoring it for a second before I moved inside.

She gripped my shoulders for balance, one of her hands grabbing the back of my neck. She was panting, and I could feel her hard nipples through the shirt. "I've never had anyone bare before you," she confessed.

"Me neither." Now that I had, I wondered how the hell I could ever go back. The feeling was addictive. *She* was addictive. I put the head of my cock inside her, letting it slip and slide, as I tasted her skin with the tip of my tongue. "You feel that?" I growled.

She gave me a moan that was both pleasure and frustration. "I feel *everything*," she said. "Everything you do. Give me more, Max."

I moved my hips and pushed further into her. She was tighter than last night, all heat and incredible friction. I braced myself against the counter, my muscles tense, and slid in all the way. Her fingers dug into my shoulders and she tilted her head away from me, giving me better access to her neck. "More," she said.

But I moved slow. This was different from before, here on my kitchen counter, with the cloudy sunlight slanting into the room through my curtains and the coffee maker ticking on the counter behind me. I savored her this time, the smell of her skin—rubbed-off coconut lotion and sleepy, aroused woman—and the quiet sounds in her throat. I savored the feel of her around me, the slickness of her skin where it touched mine, the taut muscles I could feel in her legs gripping me, in her arms holding herself up. There was only one thing missing. "Take your shirt off," I told her.

She paused for a second, the words registering in her brain. "What?"

"Take it off or I won't make you come."

I gripped her waist so she wouldn't fall, and in one graceful movement she pulled the t-shirt off and tossed it away. "Better?"

"Hell, yes." It was. I had never seen a woman with skin like Gwen's, with breasts that moved like hers, that hot, heavy shape tipped with dark pink nipples. Now I had her perfectly naked and I was inside her, and I gripped her more tightly and moved a little faster, a little harder.

She squirmed against me, trying to buck into me. "*Max*," she complained.

"Be quiet," I told her, throbbing inside her. "I told you you're going to come, and you will."

"I just—I—"

"Ssh," I said. "Like this." I reached a hand between us. I had done this the first time, by instinct, and now I did it again. I slid my thumb over her clit, and then I simply held it there, unmoving, letting the friction do the work. The sounds she started making told me I was doing it right. "Damn it," I said as she got closer, as I felt my body start to let go. "Come on my cock. Just like that."

I felt it when the orgasm rippled through her, just like I'd felt it last night. She was quieter this time, her cry strangled in her throat, like it had taken her by surprise. I was at the end of my rope; I came too, a rush of relief through my whole body, my balls tight. We stilled for a second, my mouth still against the skin of her neck.

Then I felt her tighten up. Her back, her shoulders, her legs around my hips. She lost that relaxed, just-come feeling and her hands slid down my shoulders, her palms pushing at me. "I should clean up," she said.

I let her go and she slid off the counter, picking up the t-shirt and walking away to the bathroom without a word.

I stood there, feeling stripped—not just of my clothes, but of everything. I had never in my life had sex like that. I had never come close. And I might not know everything about her, but if I had to guess, neither had she.

Something was wrong.

I reached to the floor and pulled my boxers back on, so at least I wouldn't have my dick hanging out when I got stomped on. Because I had the sudden feeling that was about to happen.

She came out of the bedroom minutes later, fully dressed, her purse slung over her shoulder. "I have to go," she said, her voice neutral, her eyes barely touching me before glancing away again.

"Yeah?" I said, keeping my own voice neutral. "Where do you have to go?"

She was pulling her sandals on. "I have to go to work, Max."

Fuck. The idea made me quietly insane, but if there was one thing I was good at, it was hiding my feelings. I looked at the clock. "Yeah? You have to strip at ten o'clock in the morning?"

She finished with her sandal and stood, her cheeks red. "No, I have to go home and shower and clean up, and then eat something and have a nap, because it's going to be a long night and I'll be out late. I have three gigs tonight."

I nearly choked. Three? We'd just fucked a minute ago, I'd been inside her, feeling her come, and she had to take her clothes off for three different parties? "You're in demand, huh?" I said.

Something in my voice made her go on the defensive. "I have to make money," she said, the words snapping with anger that I didn't think was directed at me. "This is my job. I'm good at it—the best. And I like it."

"No, you don't." The words were out of my mouth before I considered them, and they only made her angrier.

"You don't get a say in what I like or I don't like," she said, her voice tight. "You don't get a say in what I do, either."

I should be pissed. Hurt, maybe. But to me, the words sounded like a line she'd used one too many times, so I shrugged. "I get it," I said. "You're playing games."

Her cheeks went redder. "What the hell does that mean?"

"Just that it won't work with me."

"You're full of shit, you know that?" She picked up her purse again. "I'm leaving."

You want to know if it bothered me? It did. It really

fucking did. I might not see her again, and I was starting to understand exactly what that meant, exactly what I would be missing. "You think this was a one-time thing?" I asked her as she headed for the door, my voice gruff.

She paused, glancing back at me, and for a split second I saw it in her face—uncertainty, and something else, something that looked like panic and sadness mixed together. Then she pushed the expression away and went blank again. "Did you think it was otherwise?" she said.

I couldn't quite figure it out. It was going too fast, and her signals were too jumbled, and as usual my words weren't working for me. "I guess not," I said, some unnamed emotion bubbling up from deep inside me, fueling me. I had no patience for games. "But if you walk out, don't call me. You're the first woman I fucked since getting my leg blown off, and I'm not in the mood to be jerked around."

She paled, and her lips parted in shock.

I shrugged. "You want to humiliate me, I get that. I've been through worse. But somehow, I don't think you do. Something's pissing you off, and you don't have the guts to own it. So I'm gonna go get dressed, because I'm tired of having this conversation naked, and I've got shit to do today." I headed for the bedroom door. "See ya, Gwen."

She was quiet for a minute, and I was already in the bedroom when I heard the front door close behind her.

Chapter 11

Gwen

HE BLEW ME OFF.

Max Reilly blew. Me. Off.

No man did that to me. Ever. Sure, I'd been a bit rude—okay, bitchy maybe—and sure, I'd been unfair. The truth was, after that unreal sex session on his kitchen counter, I'd felt completely out of my depth. Like something was happening that I couldn't control. It had seemed fun and exciting, being out of control the night before. But after that—God, it had been so intense—I had felt like I was careening down a hill with no brakes. Like there was no way this was going to end well.

And then I'd remembered my job.

Like Trent had suggested, I'd taken extra gigs to help pay my back rent. Three of them in one night. I'd never had a problem getting naked—it was what I did. But suddenly, after being naked with Max, the idea made me queasy. Being naked with Max was *nothing* like being naked with anyone else. They were on two different planets. And since work-naked paid the bills and Max-naked didn't, I'd had to make a choice.

At least, that's what I told myself.

I got myself home, entering my tiny apartment on orgasm-weakened legs, my brain still spinning. I had a rented matchbox in a high-rise building, which sounds luxurious but was anything but. It was the smallest apartment known to man, the cheapest thing I could afford without roommates. It was a single room, with a kitchen counter along one wall and a queen sized bed on the other. The bathroom door swung halfway into the main room. Even with its stingy square footage, the rent was still outrageous, and my few attempts to decorate had been so pathetic I'd simply given up.

I took a long, hot shower, then flopped on my back on my bed, staring at the ceiling. My traitorous body was still blissed out because of Max Reilly. His hands. His whole big body. His teeth on my neck. His ridiculous biceps. His smoking hot beard, which was surprisingly soft when you ran your fingertips through it, or felt the edge of it on your tongue when you licked his lip, or when he put his head between your legs and—

Damn it, damn it. I had to stop. I'd scratched my itch. I had work to do.

But hours later, after I'd rested and prepped and done my first gig, I still felt bad. Pervasively, shittily bad. I didn't want to be here, doing my Naughty Nurse routine at some guy's fiftieth birthday party (the evening's early slot, since the birthday boy wouldn't last much past ten.) I sat in my car, supposedly on my way to my second gig, but instead parked and looking at my phone, thinking about texting Max.

If you walk out, don't call me. You're the first woman I fucked since getting my leg blown off, and I'm not in the mood to be jerked around.

How long had that been for him? Years? I thought I was so goddamned tough, that my life was so fucking hard. With a few words, Max always showed me how shallow I was. How brittle. What if I pushed him too far this time? What if he was really done with me?

I surprised myself by feeling an echo of panic inside my ribcage. The thought of Max being done with me was bleak, even if I'd done my best to push him away only this morning. I was truly going crazy.

So I typed: *Are you there?*

There was half a minute of silence, and then he answered. *Yes.*

What are you doing? I wrote, because even when we were fighting, apparently, I was curious about him.

Just left the gym, he wrote back.

That gave me mental pictures of Max, muscled and sweaty, maybe wearing workout shorts and a t-shirt that was stuck to his skin. On any other guy I'd think that borderline gross, but with Max I knew that if I pushed his sweaty shirt up and inhaled, he'd smell like sex. Damn him.

At least he was talking to me. There were very few words, but at least they were there. I gritted my teeth and prepared to apologize to a man for the first time since I was eighteen. *I'm sorry about this morning,* I wrote.

There was a long, long minute of silence. I'd surprised him. Welcome to the club, because I'd surprised myself. Then he wrote, *Where are you right now?*

It didn't cross my mind to lie to him. *I'm in my car,*

between gig one and gig two.

His reply was immediate. *Ditch it. Quit. Come over.*

I put the phone down on the seat next to me, put my hands on the wheel, and leaned forward until my forehead hit the wheel. Those words were like a punch to the gut, almost physical, painful, breathtaking.

I wanted to do that. So. Bad.

I wanted to start my car and drive to South San Francisco, to Shady Oaks. I wanted to take off these uncomfortable clothes, these high heels, wash off my make-up, and curl up on Max's sofa, watching TV and breathing him in. I even wanted to listen to his grumpy arguments and non-conversations. And later, when we were both tired, I wanted to climb into his bed with him and have sex in every possible combination until neither of us could move.

But that wasn't reality. I'd lose my paycheck, lose my apartment. I couldn't just give up my life to rely on a man. That was the epitome of stupid. I'd wanted that once, and it had turned out so badly I still couldn't even speak his name.

And that was what it came down to, wasn't it? That was why I was here, eight years after The Bad Thing happened, sitting alone in a car in a naughty nurse outfit, lonely and sick of it. Because of The Bad Thing when I was eighteen. The thing I still hadn't gotten over.

Thinking about it made me cold, so I had the strength to pick up the phone again and type, *Sorry, I can't. I need the money. I have to go.*

Then I turned off my phone.

Chapter 12

Max

"YOU GOT ANY GOOD CLOTHES?" MY BEST FRIEND Devon Wilder asked me on the phone.

"I don't know. Maybe," I said, rifling through my cupboards for some peanut butter to put on my toast. I thought about Devon's court dates, my dad's funeral. "Probably."

"Wear them," he said. "You're coming to the theater with me and Olivia in two hours."

"The hell I am," I said, just because I was ornery and the thought of putting on nice clothes was intimidating. "It's Friday night. Maybe I have plans."

"Yeah," Devon said in obvious disbelief. "What are you doing right now, Max?"

"Eating peanut butter toast for dinner," I admitted.

"Exactly. So put on some nice shit. I'll even send a limo, because that's what we're doing for Liv's sister."

"Wait," I said, putting the peanut butter jar down on the counter. "Liv's sister is coming?" I knew she had a sister, but I'd never seen her.

"Liv insisted," Devon said. "She wants me and her sister to get along, do something nice. So I got a theater box for *Macbeth*, but it has four seats. So I'm bringing you."

I didn't like this one bit, though I loved *Macbeth*. "What exactly is my purpose in this box?" I asked him. "Just so I'm clear. Is my purpose to be a buffer between you and Olivia's sister in case it's awkward? Or am I just supposed to round out the third wheel?"

"Jesus," Devon said. "You're still doing the overthinking thing. I thought you had a shrink for that."

Devon Wilder was literally the only man on the planet who had a license to make shrink jokes at me, and that was only because I'd known him since I was six and I literally owed him my life. "I do," I said. "I just hate surprises."

"There are no surprises," Devon said. "Your purpose, since you asked, is to show up and watch *Macbeth* like the nerd that you are. I'm going to guess you've already read it, right?"

"Since I'm semi-literate, unlike some people, yes I have," I said. I had to get him back for the shrink joke.

"Then get dressed, Max, and be ready in an hour," Devon said. And since he knew that my anxiety was a real thing, not some figment of my imagination, he added, "It'll be easy. Liv's sister is nice. You don't have to talk to anyone else. Just come out with us and watch the play."

"Is the sister hot?" I asked suspiciously. I'd never known Devon to give a shit about my love life, but he was domesticated now, so who knew? Maybe he wanted a setup, which I would avoid like the plague.

"No comment," Devon said, which meant yes, and also that Olivia was in the room with him.

I flinched. I didn't want a night with a hot woman, since I'd already been mostly dumped by the hottest woman in San Francisco. Still, Devon was my best friend. In my head, I asked Dr. Weldman what to do, and he said I should go, so I said, "Okay, I'll get ready."

I found a pair of dark dress pants, and a pair of dark shoes. The drape of the material was a little off on my leg— jeans always looked better—but it wasn't enough to matter. I found a gray dress shirt and a belt, but since it was warm out I left off the jacket and tie. Maybe, with five million bucks in the bank, I should learn to wear a jacket and tie one of these days. Today was not that day.

I checked myself in the mirror. Not bad, but my beard was getting out of hand. I had just finished giving it a trim when I realized the limo would be pulling up any minute. A limousine at Shady Oaks was an invitation for the driver to get mugged, hit on, or sold some terrible drugs, so I grabbed my wallet and hustled down the corridor as fast as my leg would go.

And it was there, waiting for me, right in front of the front entrance. As I got in, I had two crazy thoughts at once: first, that this was how rich people live; and second, that technically I was one of those rich people. Technically I could have bought my own theater box and ordered my own limo. I could have bought a thousand-dollar suit for the occasion. Technically, I could leave Shady Oaks tomorrow for something better.

Instead of the usual anxiety the thought brought on, I contemplated it calmly on the ride into San Francisco, downtown to the theater. Five million dollars. I'd used some of it to pay off my debts—debts that had been insurmountable, but had cost me only a fraction of that money. And in true Max Reilly fashion, I'd pretended that the rest of it didn't exist, because it was too much change at once, and I hadn't been able to think about it. It was like a building so big that you had to back up and up and up before you could really see the whole thing. If you stood at the foot of the Empire State Building, all you saw when you looked up was metal and clouds.

But now, I thought maybe I could see it. I could think about things I wanted to do. Some of the small things for myself—my leg was showing some wear and tear, and now I could afford a new one, which was far from cheap. A new apartment in a nicer area.

But alongside that were the things I could do for other people. And at the top of that list was the idea that I could help Gwen give the finger to her bosses at the strip-o-gram place. *I need the money,* she'd texted me last night. But no, she didn't. Not if she let me help.

The question was, how to do it? Gwen put on a good show, but she was touchy, and she was proud. I recognized it when I saw it, because I was the same fucking way.

But Devon, with his tattoo that said *No Time,* had it right. Life was too short to be wasting time on this kind of shit. Not when you could be out there, actually doing something for someone.

I'd believed in that once—in going out and doing good in the world. It was why I'd enlisted, why I'd fought long and hard in Afghanistan. And then it had all disappeared. It had been incinerated by that IED, along with my leg, my confidence, and most of my mental health. But I'd spent long enough in fear and anxiety. Maybe it was time to go get something done again.

But first, I had to be brave enough for the theater.

When the limo pulled up in front of the theater, I got out and made my way through the crowd milling on the sidewalk. The show was to begin in thirty minutes, and the excitement was building. I hadn't bothered looking up the play online—it was *Macbeth*, what else was there to say?—but from the look of the crowd, it was a high-end production. Women were in swanky cocktail dresses, men in suits. I'd half expected a bunch of hipsters or intellectuals, showing up for their favorite Shakespeare play. I should have known that Devon would pick something better than that.

The box office knew who I was when I gave them my name—Devon Wilder's guest—and let me through. I found myself in the lobby, which was lush and red-carpeted, complete with sweeping staircase that led up to the orchestra level. There was a crowd in here too, and I took a deep breath, tried to keep focus. Crowds could be bad for guys with PTSD. I just had to find Devon, Olivia, and Olivia's sister, and we could go to the box where it was quieter, where I had less chance of an episode.

I spotted Devon almost immediately. He was hard to miss: tall, dark-haired, wearing a charcoal suit that fit him like a glove. He was standing with Olivia, who was one of those women who was quietly, smashingly gorgeous—maybe not the kind of woman who would get a modeling contract off the bat, but the kind you could look at for days without getting tired. She was slender, smaller than Devon, her gorgeous body encased in a simple, classy black dress, her dark curls set loose over her shoulders and down the middle of her back. Devon had said something, and she was looking up at him, smiling with wry humor.

Standing next to her was Gwen.

I noticed her and stopped walking just as Devon pulled his gaze from Olivia and turned around. "Max," he said.

Olivia turned, but I barely noticed. It was Gwen I saw, wearing a dark red wine-colored dress, that just barely showed her shoulders and ended at the knee. A classy dress that nonetheless made her look sexier than any other woman in the room. She'd tied her blonde hair up at the sides, clipping them back so that strands trailed down over her back and her neck. She turned and looked at me, and her expression fell. There was no other way to describe it.

Now that the two women stood side by side, I could see it. It wasn't something you'd ordinarily notice, since Olivia was dark and Gwen was fair. But when they stood together, you could see the resemblance in their cheekbones, in the set of their chins. They were the same height. They had the same perfect, slender legs. They were sisters.

Gwen was Olivia's sister.

I quickly ran that through my brain, calculating how the hell I could have known this. I came up dry. I could see in Gwen's stricken expression that she was doing the same thing.

But no. There was no way that Olivia's sister and Devon's best friend could have known each other when she'd knocked on my door.

I stepped forward. Devon was saying something—introducing us, maybe—but as usual, my words didn't work the way I wanted them to. I looked at Gwen and said, "Your last name is Maplethorpe?"

Because, yeah. We'd had sex three times, plus part of a

blow job, and I didn't know her last name. I'd never asked.

Smooth, Max. Real smooth. You really know your way around the ladies.

Gwen was just as shocked. "*You're* the hot bearded guy?" she said to me.

That gave me pause. "Which hot bearded guy?"

"The one who lives across the way from Olivia."

I was still trying to figure it out. "I don't live across from Olivia. She moved out."

"But she used to live across from you," Gwen said. "In 2D."

"Um." Olivia said this loudly, getting between us, her face red. "Hi there, you two. I didn't know you knew each other."

I looked at her. "We met," I explained.

And then Gwen said the words that put it all in perspective for me.

"*By mistake,*" she said sharply.

Right. I understood. She didn't want to know me, not in public. She didn't want anyone to know what had happened. Because to her, I was an embarrassment.

Not her usual type.

So I shut it down. Slow and deliberate. I cooled off my feelings, pushed them down, made them stop. I tore my gaze away from Gwen and turned back to Devon and Olivia. "It was just one of those things," I said, shrugging. "We ran into each other at Shady Oaks."

Devon was looking at me with that unflinching gaze of his, and it felt like he could see everything. He probably could, but it didn't matter. I put my hands in my pockets and looked back at him.

He cut me some slack and turned to Olivia. "You think he's a hot bearded guy?" he said, his voice deceptively calm.

She groaned in embarrassment. "Thanks a lot, Gwen," she said to her sister, and then, to Devon: "He *is*. It was just an objective observation. It doesn't *mean* anything."

I managed to smile at her. I liked Olivia. She had smarts and so much guts that Devon never intimidated her. "Thanks," I told her. "I'm complimented. Are we going to go find this box, or what?"

I looked at Gwen while I said it. Her cheeks were slightly flushed, her posture rigid. She was flustered. And suddenly, everything was clear to me.

She was scared. She thought she could pretend this wasn't happening between us. She thought I would actually believe that we were a mistake. That we were done. That she could use her fear to make me walk away.

She actually thought I'd walk away.

She was wrong.

Chapter 13

Gwen

I WAS STILL IN SHOCK AS WE WALKED TO THE THEATER'S wide staircase and started up toward our box. Max was Devon's friend? His best friend? That was what Olivia had said—that Devon was bringing his best friend. I felt like everything was being moved in front of my eyes, things I thought I knew, like coming home to your apartment and seeing the furniture rearranged.

Max had said he was from LA. Devon, I knew, had had a long, checkered career, most of it criminal, in both LA and San Francisco before inheriting his money. If they were best friends, there must be a side of Max that I hadn't seen. A side that had maybe done some of the things Devon did. Lived the life Devon had. The Max I knew was a recluse, quiet, dateless, reading his books and mostly hiding from the world.

There was obviously more to Max than I thought.

The men preceded us up the stairs, walking slowly alongside the crowd that was moving with us, Max with his distinctive gait as he ascended the stairs. I watched as

Devon's head bent close to Max's. They were the same height, though Max was bigger than Devon, heavier with muscle because of all his time at the gym. Devon was powerful, but he was muscle packed tight, quick and lethal. Max was the guy you'd hire as a bouncer for his lumberjack shoulders and arms.

Max said something back to Devon, just a word or two, and Devon leaned closer, talking again, gesturing briefly with one hand. I could see it in that moment, their intimacy, friends who had known each other a long time. Neither was saying much in number of words, but it was obvious their conversation was intent, Devon's focus utterly on Max. As a side benefit, the two of them were basically a sex sandwich, and half the women who saw them were practically falling down the stairs as they craned their necks.

My sister grabbed my wrist and leaned close to me, mimicking Devon's posture ahead of us. "What the heck is going on?" she hissed.

I swallowed, peeled my eyes from Max—holy hell, he looked gorgeous in dress pants and a shirt, and he'd done something ridiculously sexy to his beard—and glanced at her, shrugging. "It was just a crazy coincidence," I said. "I had a gig at Shady Oaks one day, and we met."

Her big, dark eyes were wide. "And?" she prompted.

That was the million-dollar question, wasn't it? "It's complicated," I said. "It's nothing, or maybe nothing. It's just a thing, sort of. I guess." I turned to see she was staring at me like I had two heads; I had never talked about a man like that before, babbling inane phrases to fill the quiet. "Never mind," I added, apparently unable to shut up. "I'll tell you about it later. Or most of it. Sometime later. Not now."

"Holy shit," Olivia said quietly.

I sighed. "Forget it, okay?"

"Be careful, Gwen," she said in a near-whisper as we got to the top of the stairs. "Devon adores him. Just... try to be nice, okay?"

That stung. My first reaction was anger—*What do you mean, be nice?*—and then I remembered how the words *by mistake* had flown out of my mouth, and I knew I deserved it. What the hell was wrong with me? I'd always thought of myself as strong, independent, opinionated. I'd never equated those things with being a bitch. I never crossed that line unless the situation called for it. But once again, I'd just proved myself an insecure idiot when Max Reilly was around.

"There's blood and death in this, right?" Devon asked as we walked into the theater box. It was beautiful—elegant, comfortable, completely private, with an unparalleled view of the stage. Below us, the crowd was taking their seats, the hum of conversation classy and excited. It had been years since I'd been to the theater, since the year I'd gone to acting school. I'd forgotten how fun it was, especially right before the curtain came up.

"Lots of blood and death," Max promised. There was a row of four seats. Olivia took the end. Devon sat next to her. I sat next to Devon—since this whole evening was supposed to be about him and I hanging out—and Max sat next to me.

He smelled good. His big arm brushed mine. The lights went low, though the curtain didn't go up yet. It was a moment of hushed silence, of almost unbearable anticipation.

Devon and Olivia were talking quietly, so I said to Max, "I wasn't trying to insult you. I was just shocked."

He shifted in his seat, and his arm brushed mine again.

It made my nipples go quietly hard under my dress. "It's fine," he said. "I seem to have that effect on you."

"The one where I behave like a bitch?"

"The one where you try to get rid of me," he corrected me. "It won't work."

I turned to stare at him, but the lights went down, and the curtain rose, and everyone applauded, and the play began.

* * *

By the intermission, I was a bundle of nerves. It wasn't just the play—which was intense, beautiful, dark, and perfectly performed. It was the fact that I'd spent over an hour sitting in the tension of the theater box, painfully aware of Max sitting next to me, watching raptly. Devon, on my other side, fidgeted more frequently, until each time Olivia put a hand lightly on his knee.

When the intermission lights went up, Max left the box without a word, presumably in search of a men's room. Olivia noticed and stood abruptly, saying she'd be right back. It took me a second to realize she was leaving me alone with Devon.

As if he was reading my mind, I caught Devon looking at me with an amused look in his green eyes. "She wants us to get along," he explained.

I frowned at him. "I thought we already did."

He shrugged. "It's important to her," he said, as if that was all the reason he needed. He nodded toward the stage. "Do you understand this play?"

"I haven't read it, but I know the story," I said. "We had

a Shakespeare course in acting school." I blinked at him, realizing what he was implying. "You didn't know the story already?"

He stared at the stage, looking deep in thought. "I don't think it's going to end well," he commented. "I think it's going to go badly for him. Don't tell me if I'm right or not."

I stared at him for another second, realizing exactly why my sister was a bit obsessed with Devon Wilder. He'd put on a suit—which looked pretty freaking good on him, I had to admit—and sat through a Shakespeare play that he'd never heard or read a word of before. *Shakespeare.* And he was *following* it, the same way any other guy would follow the latest *Fast and the Furious* movie. Anyone who took a glance at Devon Wilder's past—at his criminal record and his two years in prison for driving the getaway van after the robbery of a TV store—and thought they were dealing with an idiot would have a very big problem.

A lot of San Francisco drug dealers had learned that exact lesson when he'd shut them all down after they'd tried to blackmail him and hurt Olivia. There wasn't one of them left to threaten him now. They'd all been scooped up in a massive sweep he'd engineered with the cops.

Complicated didn't even touch Devon's surface. Like Max Reilly, his best friend.

I realized his green gaze had landed on me, and one of his eyebrows went up. "What?" he asked me.

The words popped out of my mouth. "Which one is smarter, you or Max?"

"Max," he answered immediately. "Easy. I'm usually catching up to him. You know he lent me books while I was in prison, right?"

"No. I didn't." I could picture it, though, and I liked what I saw. "From that big collection he has in his apartment?"

He glanced at me again, and I realized I'd just admitted I'd seen the inside of Max's apartment. "He hand picked the books he brought," he explained. "Usually stories of guys gone wrong and paying the price."

I looked away, trying not to laugh.

"I didn't have much else to do in there," Devon said. "He was the only person who came to see me regularly while I was inside." He leaned forward, putting his elbows on his knees, a pose that made the fine fabric of his suit do interesting things on his torso. "I owe him for a lot of things. That's just one of them."

I couldn't help it; my curiosity was killing me. "You two grew up together in LA?"

Devon nodded, still staring at the stage. "I don't know how much Olivia has told you," he said. "My brother and I pretty much had no parents. Our father split and our mother was barely around. Max's mother worked shifts, and his father was a drunk. The three of us—me, my brother Cavan, and Max—ended up together pretty much all the time."

I was quiet, trying to picture that. Devon's brother had left ten years ago, I knew from my sister, and hadn't been heard from since. Devon was trying to find him so he could claim his part of the inheritance.

"My brother Cavan was the troublemaker," Devon said, "and I was the enforcer, the guy you didn't fuck with. But Max was the sane one. The smart one. The one you always went to when you got in a jam, because he could figure a way out." He paused. "I never thought I had much of a future, and neither did Cavan. But Max was the one who was supposed to have a good life."

I looked down in my lap, thinking about Max's leg, his scars. *A case of PTSD that nearly killed me.*

"Enlisting was supposed to do it," Devon continued. "It was supposed to get him away from his toxic parents, away from LA and us, send him into a better life. When he left, he had a nice girlfriend and a good future. He was gone for four years. And then he came home."

"I've seen his leg," I said, trying not to let the words *he had a nice girlfriend* burn my stomach. "What are you getting at, Devon? Do you want me to stay away from Max? Is that it?"

He glanced over at me, amusement in his eyes again, since I'd just admitted I'd seen Max without pants on. "The opposite, actually. He needs someone to shake him up. The real Max I know has been buried ever since he came home, but I know he's in there. I think you're already bringing him out."

"How can you say that? You've seen us together for all of thirty seconds."

He actually laughed at that, the effect sort of spellbinding. "Thirty seconds are all I need, Gwen."

"Olivia thinks I might hurt him."

"Olivia doesn't know Max like I do," Devon said easily. "He's very fucking tough. He'll surprise you. I'm betting on it."

"He already surprises me," I admitted. "But you heard what I said downstairs. I'm not always a nice person, especially when it comes to him."

"Max doesn't need nice," Devon said. "Maybe once, but not right now. He needs someone to grind his gears and piss him off. I've known it for a while. I tried to shake him up myself. That's why I gave him five million dollars."

I opened my mouth, but there was a familiar deep voice in the hall, and the door opened, and Max and Olivia came in. Olivia was laughing, and Max was shaking his head, and I knew he'd said something that gave my sister the giggles. In a burst of envy, I wanted to know what it was.

Max rounded the chairs and dropped into the one next to me. "Blood and death part two, bro," he said to Devon. "You following, or do you want the picture book version?"

"This guy's dead meat," Devon said. "That part, I got. I can't read the picture book version."

"You're an embarrassment," Max said. "We can't take you anywhere."

"Blood and death," Devon said, taking Olivia's hand gently and settling in his chair. "I like it."

"So do I," Max said, and the lights went down again.

Chapter 14

Gwen

MACBETH ENDED IN ITS SYMPHONY OF TRAGEDY, but I barely paid attention. I was too stunned from the bomb Devon had dropped on me.

Five million dollars.

After the curtain went down, there was some conversation about limos, about who was getting in which one, that I barely paid attention to. Which was why I didn't know how I ended up sharing a limo home with Max, when we'd taken separate ones to the theater. All I knew was that I said my goodbyes, was handed in to the back seat of a limo, and Max got in from the other side and sat across from me.

The first thing he did was undo the button on his shirt, as if he was uncomfortable. "Okay," he said to me. "What's got you all pissed off?"

The limo moved slowly in to traffic, which was gridlocked with everyone leaving the theater, and stopped. The driver was ahead of us, behind glass. The windows were tinted. I figured now was as good a time to lay into him as any.

"Five million *dollars?*" I said.

He slumped back in his seat. "Ah, shit," he complained. "Devon told you."

I gaped at him. "You told me you'd quit your job. I believe you said, *I can afford to take some time off.* That's it. You didn't say anything about five million dollars."

"I didn't want to sound like an asshole," he said, running a hand through his hair. "That's what guys say to blondes who walk in to a bar, isn't it? *Look at me, sweetheart, I have five million bucks.*"

"But you *do,*" I said. "We've had sex three times. We've slept together. You've never brought it up?"

His cheeks flushed a little, like I'd embarrassed him, and I remembered how much I liked flustered Max. "There wasn't a good time to bring it up."

He wasn't entirely wrong. We hadn't done a ton of talking, unless you counted him saying *Come on my cock* as he rocked my world on his kitchen counter. Damn, now I was blushing too. "Fine. But you said your gym is a sweat sock, and you still go to that shitty bar."

"I like that bar."

"And you still live at Shady Oaks."

"I like Shady Oaks," he said, but then he frowned. "Okay, not really. I think I might move."

"You might move?" I said. "That's it? Five million in the bank, and you might move?"

"So I should go blow it, right?" he said, his eyes on me. "Get an expensive sports car, and a big empty mansion, and a twenty-year-old girlfriend with a boob job? Is that what I'm supposed to do?"

I crossed my arms and looked him up and down, a task I had to admit wasn't unpleasant. Damn, the man could wear dress pants and a button-down just as well as a worn-in pair of jeans. And his biceps pressed against the shirt's fabric. I couldn't picture him doing any of those things, and if any twenty-year-old with a boob job came near him right now, I'd kick her ass. "Max," I said. "You're a millionaire."

"Technically true," he agreed. "I've been trying to get my head around it, Gwen. I have. I just had things to deal with first."

My eyebrows rose. "Like what?"

"Hospital debts, for one," he said. "I was paying them the best I could, but I was never going to do it on my own. Devon was right about that. So I paid them all off with the money. I'd dropped all of my therapy, too, because of the cost, and I fixed that. There were also still debts from when my father died two years ago." He looked away from me and out the window. "He was a drunk, and a gambler, and he left things a mess. It's taken me some time to sort through everything and pay it off, since my mother died a long time ago. Then there were the costs and lawyer fees from my father's estate, which were a disaster. So forgive me if, while I was dealing with all that shit, I still lived in the same crappy apartment and went to the same crappy bar."

My chest was tight. "Jesus, Max."

He shrugged. "It's done." He seemed to think it over. "I guess I could get a haircut."

I tried to think of a single man I'd ever dated who would react to five million dollars this way. I felt like I'd been dating men from another planet. "What is it about you?" I asked him. "Every time I meet you, I learn something I didn't already know. Even if I learn it from Devon."

Max shook his head. "He did that on purpose," he said. "Told you about the money, and whatever else he told you. I think he's fucking with both of us, but mostly me."

"He's worried about you, I think," I said.

"I'm used to that." He ran a hand through his hair again, and now it was so mussed that I couldn't stand it anymore. As the limo inched through the traffic leaving the city, I kicked off my shoes and moved across the back seat, settling in a straddle on his lap.

"Oh, hell," he said, but it was half a sigh, and I felt his muscles relax.

I had to pull my dress up almost to my hips to free up my legs, and as soon as I felt his big, hard, warm thighs under me I did what I was most dying to do: I leaned forward and kissed him.

He tasted so good, like malt and something a little bit sweet, and I felt the rush of it all through my body. In minutes we were making out like teenagers, his tongue brushing mine, one of his hands on the back of my neck, the other sliding up under my dress and over my hip. I dug my fingers into his soft hair and bit his lip as I broke the kiss. "Did you miss me?" I panted into his mouth.

"Nope," he said.

"Good. Me neither," I said, and kissed him again.

As it always did, everything melted away when I was with Max. All of my jitteriness, my uncertainty, the knots I tied myself in—everything. I was drunk on him, boneless and happy as one of his big hands cupped my breast through my dress. This was going to go very dirty, very fast. Part of me wanted it to. Who would know, after all? People probably fucked in limos all the time. And I wanted Max to fuck me in one. I wanted Max to fuck me anywhere.

But I also wanted control this time, so I reached between us, unzipped his pants, and ran the palm of my hand over his cock.

"Fuck," he growled against my neck. "What are you doing?"

"Just sit still," I told him as I pulled his cock from his boxer briefs. "I have a present for you." I slid my hand up him, rubbing the head, and then down again.

"*Gwen,*" he said, jumping beneath me like I'd given him an electric shock. God, I loved it when I got that reaction.

I gently sucked his lower lip, feeling the roughness of his beard, as I did it again. "You don't like it?" I teased.

He groaned against me. "Fuck, woman."

I stroked him again, feeling every twitch of his big body beneath mine, and I had one crazy, possessive thought: *Mine.* This hot, complicated man was all mine, and I wanted to hear it. "What was it you said about not having a woman since Afghanistan?"

His teeth grazed the side of my neck. "I tell you stupid things when we fight. *Fuck.* Do that harder."

I did, but I slowed down, savoring it. Savoring him. Not just the torture I was giving him, but the pleasure. I'd never liked pleasing a man before I met Max, I realized. It had always felt like I'd lost something that the man had won. But pleasing Max was nothing like that—it was hot and incredibly fucking rewarding.

There was some come on him now, and it made my hand slick. As if reading my mind, he reached up and cupped the side of my head in his hand, looking into my eyes as I pumped him. "You still think we're a mistake?" he growled.

I couldn't do anything but tell him the truth. "No," I admitted. "I never thought that."

I stroked him again, and I watched the pure pleasure darken his eyes. "Quit stripping," he said.

"I can't," I panted.

"Gwen," he said, his voice pure blackness. "*Quit your fucking job.*"

God, he was killing me. "I'll explain later," I said. "Just come first."

He leaned forward and brushed his mouth over mine, his tongue touching me as I stroked. He was close, I could tell—his muscles were tight, his breath short. "You'll get what you want," he said. "You always do."

I was out of breath. I had never been so turned on when a man wasn't even touching me. I had nothing but the bare truth left in me. "I want to see it," I confessed.

And his voice, again, made me shiver. "No," he said darkly. "You want to swallow it."

And I did. I suddenly wanted that more than anything. I slid off his lap and onto my knees on the floor, and as the limo took the highway to South San Francisco, I swallowed every last drop.

It was wonderful.

While I was readjusting my dress and sitting back down on the seat like a normal person, Max zipped his pants and opened the window that communicated to the driver. "Just one stop," he said shortly. "Miss Maplethorpe's place." He closed the window again, sat down, and looked at me. "We're not done."

I didn't answer, but my heart tripped in my chest and my neck felt hot.

It wasn't just sex he was talking about. Max Reilly had plans. And I was about to find out what they were.

Chapter 15

Gwen

MAX LOOKED HUGE IN MY TINY APARTMENT, taking up all the space in the middle of the room. He looked around briefly, taking in everything in a glance, his expression unreadable. I turned on the lamp next to my tiny futon sofa, not ready for the scrutiny of the overhead lights.

I was shaky. Hot. Turned on, able to feel how slick and wet I was between my legs. And I was nervous. I had the feeling that the power I'd grabbed in the limo had slipped out of my hands and into his—and I gave it up willingly, which I didn't understand.

I stood in the middle of the room, watching him. He was tall and gorgeous, muscled beneath his nice clothes. His stomach was perfectly flat beneath his dress shirt, the lines unbroken where it was tucked in to his pants. He'd managed to straighten himself out better than I had; I could feel that my dress was wrinkled, my underwear damp, my skin blotched with heat.

He turned to me, his eyes dark and unreadable, and

walked toward me. *I have no idea what he's going to do*, I thought, and the idea was thrilling. Maybe he'd talk to me; maybe he'd fuck me; maybe he'd do neither. Maybe he'd simply walk past me and leave. I'd always been able to predict what a man would do, especially once I had him alone in my apartment. I could tell when he would make small talk, when he'd decide to make a move. I could tell so far ahead that I'd already decided what my reaction would be by the time he got there.

Max rounded behind me and brushed my hair off the back of my neck, exposing the zipper of my dress. Then, without a word, he unzipped it.

He didn't speak. I held still, feeling the zipper lower down my back. I had the feeling that this wasn't about sex, though my body was humming in hopeful anticipation. The few times we'd had sex, Max hadn't been like this; he'd been hot, barely restrained, as if a door he kept locked was pried open. Now he was cool, all business.

So I waited. He drew the zipper all the way down, then edged the dress off my shoulders. He held it, decorously, as I took my cue and stepped out of it. Then he draped it calmly over the back of my kitchen chair.

"Your shoes," he said, and I pushed off my heels. Now I was standing in my bare feet, wearing only my bra and panties. Max stood off to the side, regarding me. He scratched his beard.

"There's something I've been trying to figure out about you," he said.

I fought the urge to fidget. How many men had I stood in front of, wearing nothing but skimpy underwear? Hundreds, probably, in my career. But I already knew that being naked in front of Max wasn't like being naked in front of anyone else. I didn't know what this game was, but I knew I wanted to play.

"What is it?" I asked.

He was still, watching me. "I've been thinking about what you want." He stepped forward, looking at me more closely, as if I were a statue in a museum. "I wonder about it. Not just what you want in the next few minutes. I mean what you *really* want."

For some reason, my mouth went dry. No one had ever asked me that. "It isn't complicated," I managed.

"I think it is." His finger touched my bra strap, and my nipples hardened. If he noticed, he didn't let on. "I think you tell everyone a story about yourself, but it isn't true. And I think you tell that story even to yourself, and you tell yourself you believe it. That's what makes it hard for me to see."

"And what about you?" I went on the defensive, because the scrutiny was too much. "You think you can analyze me, but what do you want?"

"A lot of things," he said, hooking his finger gently under my bra strap and drawing it down my arm. "Mostly you. All to myself. Without sharing."

My stomach flipped. "You decided that awfully recently."

"No. I decided it the minute I unzipped your dress the first time, while you sat in my lap. That's what you don't see about me. I never fuck a woman I don't want."

"So you haven't wanted a woman in four years?"

He sighed and moved to my other bra strap. "I've wanted plenty of women, believe me. But most women don't want a mangled mess with a fucked-up head. Until you."

"Stop it," I said. "You're none of those things."

"I am," he said calmly. "I own it. That's why we're not talking about me. We're talking about you." He slid the other bra strap down, and his voice gentled. "I think you wanted something once, and you didn't get it. So you decided you didn't want anything anymore."

They cut like a sharpened blade, those words. They hurt, and my first reaction was to hurt him back. "Fuck you, Max."

"What was it?" he asked, unfazed by my hostility. My bra straps were both down now, but he made no move to remove my bra. "What did you want so much? Tell me what it was."

"God, you are so fucking clueless." The words came out without thinking. I had to hurt before the hurt came to me—I always had to. "You think you're so smart, but you don't know me at all." I glared at him. "It was just a few fucks, Max. That's all it was. Maybe it seemed like more to you, because it had been so long. But I can tell you that it wasn't more to me. There's a lineup of men who want me. I could pick any one."

He watched me with his dark eyes, and then he unbuttoned one cuff, rolling the sleeve back over his muscled arm. "That's how you're going to play it, is it?" he said, his voice deceptively casual. "That's what you're going to say?"

"Yes. I strip because I like it." Those words came out hard—they were such a lie I could barely choke them out of my throat. "I like it when men watch me and they can't have me. I like making them hard. I like knowing that they think of me when they jerk off at night. That I'm the one they'll never have." I choked out another lie. "Just like I'm the one you'll never have."

He just shook his head, rolling his other sleeve up. "You just swallowed my come in the limo fifteen minutes ago," he pointed out. "You loved it. You expect me to believe that?"

The memory of that was still so fresh, so consuming, that I couldn't speak for a second. Then I said, "I was playing with you."

"You were never playing with me." Now there was an undercurrent of anger in his voice, controlled but unmistakable. "You just think you were. Now go to the bed."

I gaped at him. "You actually think you're going to fuck me?"

He shook his head again. "I'm not remotely going to fuck you, Gwen. That would be too easy. Now go to the bed."

I did it. That was how messed up I was, how badly I wanted to know what came next. I walked over to the bed, pretending that my knees weren't almost shaking. This was the strangest thing I'd ever done, but saying those words, listening to him, letting the truth come out—it was so exciting it was almost unbearable. "Okay, now what?" I snapped.

He had followed me. He put a hand on my shoulder and turned me so I faced the side of the bed. He hooked his fingers in my panties at my hips, pushing them to the floor; I wondered if he could see how wet I was, if he even noticed. Then he put a big, warm hand on my back and pressed me gently until I was bent over, my palms braced on the bed.

What was this? It wasn't sex. I wanted it to be sex—despite my brave words, if he'd fucked me I would have given in, and I would have come in minutes. But he didn't even take his clothes off. He ran his hand up my back, unhooked my bra, let it fall to the bed. Then he ran his hand around my waist, over my hip, holding me in place.

"What are you doing?" I said. My voice was shaky. His touch was making me crazy.

He leaned forward and his beard brushed my skin as he spoke. "I'm showing you who is playing who."

The first spank hit my ass out of the blue, and I jumped. He held me in place so I wouldn't lose my balance.

"*Ow!*" I shouted.

He spanked me again, and it was a shock of pain. His hand was big, his arm powerful, and the sting was sharp on my skin.

"*Max!* What are you—"

"Be quiet," he said. And then he added the most curious instruction: "Just feel it."

I closed my eyes. He was bracing me with one arm over my bent hips; his hold wasn't even tight. I could have pushed him off, gotten away. I could even have kicked him or punched him, kneed him in the balls. Instead I stilled and waited in a crazy sort of curiosity.

The third hit made me gasp. The pain was wild, sudden, flushing through my skin before evaporating again. Anger flooded through me, sudden and powerful, like poison in my veins—not anger at Max, but anger at *everything*. It was like the pain had released it from where I kept it locked down. I felt like screaming.

He spanked me again, and the sadness came up. The self-pity. I didn't sob, but I felt wet tears on my cheeks, as if everything that needed to come out was finally being let go. And with the next spank came the lust, the pain blooming between my legs, down my ass and the backs of my thighs. The lust only escalated with the next hit, my body clenching and empty. I wanted him inside me. I couldn't be happy until he was there. I wanted to fuck him for hours.

He paused, rubbing his palm over my sore ass, seeming to assess me. It made my skin tingle. I was panting as hard as if I'd run a mile.

"We done?" he asked me.

"Yes," I said.

"Are you gonna behave?"

I should have been insulted, but I knew what he was doing. It was deliberate. He was letting me let go—*making* me let go. "Yes," I said.

Then he was gone, and I took a breath and straightened. In a second he was back with my bathrobe, which he must have found on the hook inside my closet door. I hadn't even heard him look.

He put the bathrobe over my shoulders and helped me into the sleeves. When I had tied the belt, he said, "Talk."

I sat on the bed—gently, on my sore butt—and looked down at my lap. The words came in a rush, the same way the emotions had.

"When I was eighteen, I got pregnant," I told him. "It wasn't on purpose, but once I knew what was happening… I wanted it. I wanted to keep it. I thought I loved my boyfriend. I thought he would agree."

The bed sagged as Max sat down next to me, listening.

I shook my head, remembering. "I was stupid. I was eighteen, and I had no idea what love was, but I thought I did. I thought my boyfriend would be as happy as I was, that we'd make a life. It was a silly fantasy. He was horrified when he found out. We fought. He wanted me to get rid of the baby. When I wouldn't, he said he needed space, time to figure things out. Basically, he dumped me." I risked a glance at Max. He was watching me, his dark eyes steady on me, listening. I looked down in my lap again. "He was eighteen, too, and we'd been careful, so he was terrified. I see that now, though I didn't see it then. It didn't matter, anyway. Three weeks later I miscarried. I was just under three months along." I took a breath, letting it go deep into my lungs. "That was eight years ago, and I've never been able to talk about it until right now."

He made no comment. "Does your mother know?"

"Yes," I said. Normally I felt unbearable pain even thinking about this, but now I just felt light, like I could float away. "Olivia, too. She's a year older than me, and there was no hiding what was going on. Both of them know what happened. But I played it down, and I've never talked about it again to either of them. They both think that I just dealt with it and moved on. They both think I'm so strong, that nothing gets me down, that I just picked myself up and kept going. My mother worries about Olivia, about whether she's happy, but she never worries about me. She always says it's because she doesn't have to."

"They're wrong," Max said simply.

The words felt like they invaded my chest and squeezed it. I glanced at him again. He was watching me, that familiar frown between his eyebrows. "I put up a pretty good show," I said. "But my life ever since then…" I looked around my apartment, ran a hand through my hair. "I've never admitted it to myself, but I do what I do because it makes me feel like I'll never hurt like that again. Like nothing could possibly tear me apart and break me down. Not a man, not a job, not anything."

"I get that," Max said, and he stood up and crossed my

tiny apartment to my fridge, where he found a half-drunk bottle of white wine. "Now tell me about this problem you have with your job," he said, his voice growling as he found two glasses and pulled the cork off the bottle.

Considering I had just told him the worst thing that had ever happened to me, the thing that had ruined my life, it wasn't an emotional scene. But I realized that was what I wanted. I didn't even feel like crying; I felt calm, able to handle it for the first time, as if after all these years I could finally deal. It seemed that even when he was spanking my ass, Max was slaying my demons. He handed me a glass of wine, and I told him about Trent, and how he was keeping money from my paycheck, threatening me. How he wanted me to work his exclusive party, supposedly to get my money back. A party he himself would attend.

And Max listened to that too, standing a few feet away from me, until all of the words had spilled out. Then he downed his glass of wine in one shot and put the glass down on my small table. The frown between his brows had turned into a full-on grizzly bear scowl.

"Okay," he said. "I'm going to handle this. You get some rest."

My jaw dropped open. "What do you mean, you're going to handle it?"

"Exactly what I say. Drink your wine. Go to sleep. Do whatever you like. Just don't worry about this anymore. Oh, and don't take any more gigs."

"But tomorrow's Saturday," I protested. "Saturday nights are my best moneymaking nights."

"Gwen," he said, exasperated, "forget about the fucking money. That's an order."

113

I stood up, because he was turning and striding for the door. "Where are you going?"

"To handle some shit," he replied. "I'll talk to you later."

"Wait!" He stopped, and turned to look at me. His expression was just barely composed, but I could see it—he was furious, though not at me.

I didn't want him to leave. I wanted to talk to him. I wanted to thank him. I wanted to have sex with him. I wanted to sleep. I wanted all of those things at the same time, so all I managed to say was, "Are you going to beat him up?"

For a second Max's eyes blazed, and I realized what a very, very bad idea it was to cross a man who had already seen more, and done more, than most people did in a lifetime. "That would be very fucking fun," he said, his voice chilled, "I admit it. But no." His eyes blazed again. "He isn't going to heal from what I have in mind."

He turned, and then he was gone, letting the door fall shut softly behind him.

I was a different woman than I'd been an hour ago. Other than that, it was as if he'd never been.

Chapter 16

Max

"**I** REALLY DON'T MISS SHADY OAKS," DEVON SAID.

I pulled up a tattered lawn chair and sat in it. We were in the central courtyard at Shady Oaks, sitting around the dried-up pool, which was filled with leaves and old cigarette butts instead of water. It was eleven o'clock on Saturday night, and I dropped a six-pack onto the concrete between us.

"Give me one of those." Ben Hanratty, Devon's lawyer, pulled his half-wrecked lawn chair closer and grabbed for a beer. Since he'd inherited an estate worth a billion dollars, Devon was now the kind of guy to have a lawyer—but, being Devon, he didn't have the usual kind. Ben was in his thirties, with dirty blond hair and a scruff of beard. Tonight he was wearing a black hooded sweatshirt, dirty jeans, and motorcycle boots. He looked like the president of the local MC on his night off, but he was actually a whip-smart lawyer who took no shit. He'd worked for Devon before the inheritance, had defended him in his prison case, and his loyalty to his client was without question.

"Is there a reason we had to meet here?" Devon asked me, cracking his own beer. He was dressed like Ben, in old jeans and a dark green Henley beneath a battered leather jacket. Together they looked like they were about to mug someone or take some old lady's purse. "I thought when I moved out of my apartment and gave it to you, I'd never have to see this place again."

"Especially after Olivia moved out," Ben agreed. Olivia had lived in the apartment across the way until she'd moved into Devon's house in Diablo last month. "I see the place hasn't improved since I saw it last."

I picked up my own beer. "The place hasn't improved since it was built in the sixties," I said. "What did you expect?"

"That we'd meet somewhere with actual chairs," Devon said, squirming in his lawn chair. "And maybe a roof."

"You've gotten soft," I teased him. "Shady Oaks used to be good enough for you."

In one of the corridors above us, a cloud of pot smoke wafted from an apartment. Someone laughed. Two women came into the complex and crossed the courtyard, weaving and giggling. One of them catcalled us, loudly. Devon glanced over his shoulder at them and turned back to me, shrugging. "It's a dump," he observed. "So what do you want us here for?"

"Gwen has a problem," I said, "with the piece of shit she works for."

Devon's eyebrows shot upward. "Gwen?"

"The stripper?" Ben asked.

"Listen," I said, and I laid it out for them. I felt myself getting angry even as I talked about it, but I kept myself under control. This meeting was about getting shit done, not giving in to my emotions.

Even if it would feel really, really good to make this Trent guy sorry.

When I finished talking, Devon gripped his beer. "She hasn't told Olivia about any of this," he said. "She doesn't know a thing."

"Gwen is proud," I said. I could relate. "She's embarrassed that she got into it. She wanted to deal with this herself. But she can't."

"Which she admitted to you," Devon observed sharply. "When exactly?"

After I spanked her ass red, I thought, but I said, "Never mind that. The point is, something needs to be done about this situation. Gwen could sue him for her back pay, but she can't afford a lawyer."

Devon's voice was low and dry, the way it was when he was starting to get quietly, hotly angry. "She can now."

"That would be me," Ben broke in. He put his beer down and rubbed his hands together in anticipation. "He can't withhold her pay like that. It's so fucking illegal it gives me a hard-on. I'd sue him for free, just to put a hook in his balls, but Devon won't let me."

"Nope," Devon said.

Ben shrugged. "I'll take your money if you insist. But something tells me that's not what we're going to do."

"Correct," I said. "So we sue him, so what? It takes months before it goes to court, and in the meantime he declares bankruptcy or leaves the state. Gwen never gets her money, and he starts up somewhere else. We need a better plan."

"Which you've already thought of," Devon said, his green eyes gleaming in the dark. He swigged his beer. "Spill it, Max. Do we put him out of business?"

"I thought of that, too. Still not good enough," I said. "He just comes up with a new name and pops up somewhere else, takes advantage of a new roster of women. No. I want this guy finished. As in, completely finished."

"I like the sound of this," Ben said, laughing.

"I hired an investigator," I told them. "A fellow vet. I know him from the bar I go to. It only took him a few hours today to find a few things we can use."

"Such as?" Devon said.

I took a long drink of my beer. "First of all, he's behind on his back rent in the office he rents. He's about to get evicted. The building itself is underwater, and the landlord is desperate to sell."

Devon's voice was still angry. "How much?"

"He'll unload the whole place for ninety grand," I said. This was pocket change to Devon—and to me, now. We exchanged a look. "But that's not all. I started wondering, if he's docking all of these women's pay, what is he using the money for? Not his rent, obviously—he's not paying that either. So where the hell is the money going?" I looked at them. "So I had my investigator dig. This Trent guy lives in a low-rent apartment he inherited from his parents. He doesn't have any alimony or child support payments. He doesn't have any big debts on the books. He doesn't gamble that my guy could find, or go on trips, and he isn't supporting some rich girlfriend. We couldn't find where the money was going, but we could see everywhere that it *isn't* going. So what does that tell you?"

Devon nodded, following where I was going immediately. "Drugs," he said.

"It has to be," I agreed.

In the darkness, Devon laughed a low laugh. "There's nothing I love more than putting a drug dealer out of business."

After he'd inherited his money, some drug dealers from Devon's past had tried to blackmail him to pay up by threatening Olivia. Devon had responded by wiping most of them out in one of the city's biggest-ever busts. It wasn't permanent, of course—these guys were like rats—but still, it was a pretty doomed lowlife dealer who crossed paths with Devon Wilder.

Ben finished his beer and tossed the empty bottle into the garbage-filled pool. "I'm in," he said. "I live for this shit."

"We'll split the building," Devon said, looking at me. "Give me a day and I can get it done. I want to do it for Olivia. She's going to be upset when she hears what her sister's been through. And then we'll take care of the rest."

I drained my own beer and tossed the bottle, hearing it smash in the empty pool. I didn't want to go to bed yet, alone in my apartment, wondering if Gwen had followed my instructions tonight and turned down any stripping gigs. "Okay," I said.

Devon was watching me. "You're going to a lot of trouble for someone you just met by accident and won't talk about," he said.

I decided I owed him at least a little truth. "We have a thing," I said.

That made him laugh. "You think? You both looked shocked as hell at the theater the other night. You have a thing, and you didn't even know her last name?"

"No last name?" Ben whistled. "Nice."

"It didn't come up," I said, and winced, looking at Devon's expression. "It isn't like me, I know. It just sort of happened." *And it keeps happening,* I thought. *Unless she's done with me.*

"Well, I like it," Devon said. "Gwen doesn't need some wimpy-ass guy, which according to Olivia is the kind of guy she usually dates. She makes them jump through hoops to get anywhere near her. Looks like you've already passed that test."

"Don't be so sure," I said. "I pretty much piss her off."

"Fine with me," Devon said, getting up. "Just give me a warning so I can take cover when the fireworks start."

Chapter 17

Gwen

B Y MONDAY, I FELT BETTER THAN I HAD IN AS LONG as I could remember. Maybe ever.

I'd spent the weekend doing something crazy: almost nothing. I'd slept, and watched Netflix, and ate whatever I wanted. I took long baths and did my nails and thought about maybe going out to shop, and then I went to sleep again.

And I stayed dressed. I wore whatever I wanted, which turned out to be the same yoga pants and sweatshirt for both days. I left my thongs and high heels and skimpy costume dresses in a pile in the corner, and I didn't look at them.

Max was right. I hated my fucking job. It was time to quit. I never wanted to do it again. There had to be a way.

I thought about it as I stood in front of the bathroom mirror after my shower on Monday morning. I looked at my body through the mist for a long time, trying on the idea of not stripping anymore. Of my body as just mine, instead of a way to make a living. I could wear underwear that covered my whole ass, and no bra. I could stop waxing between my legs, let the hair grow in. I could eat pizza and gain five pounds. Ten. As long as *I* liked my body, what the hell would it matter?

I liked the idea—so much, it scared me.

I'm done, I thought, looking at my body, running my hands over my hips. *No one ever has to look at my body again, except me.*

And then, the inevitable next thought: *And Max.*

Max didn't care what I wore, nor would he care if I gained ten pounds. My ass had been red until Sunday morning. A man with that much passion wouldn't care if I went up a dress size. Actually, he'd probably fuck me harder.

That, I thought, feeling my blood pump hot beneath my skin. *I want that.* It was exhilarating, and terrifying. I hadn't wanted anything in a long time, because the last time I had, it had been taken away from me.

I put on jeans and a t-shirt and called Olivia. "Hey," I said when she answered. "Are you at work? Want to do lunch? We can include wine. No, scratch that—let's just do the wine."

"I worked an exhibit Saturday night, so I have today off," she said, referring to the art gallery she worked for. "And you're in a good mood."

"I am." I looked out the window of my tiny condo, trying to get a read on the weather, since I hadn't left the place in two days. "I'm quitting stripping."

"Well, hallelujah," she said. "I've been hoping you'd do that for years. But, um, there's something going on."

I straightened away from the window. "What do you mean?"

"Devon's been up to something all weekend," she said.

"He won't tell me what it is, but when he's cagey like this, I know it's something big. He had nonstop meetings yesterday, and he was already gone when I woke up this morning. I just texted him and asked him what the hell he was up to, and he said that he and Max are getting your back pay."

Oh, shit. "Devon and Max are getting my back pay?"

"What does that mean?" Olivia said. "Does that Trent creep owe you money?"

"Sort of," I said, and then remembered that it didn't matter anymore. "Yes. He owes me a lot of pay."

"And you didn't tell me?" She sounded hurt.

"I know. I'm an idiot. I confronted him about it last week and he told me to get a lawyer."

"Well, you got one better," she said. "You got Devon, and Max, and probably Ben. This, I have to see."

* * *

We went to the Candy Cane offices together. The first thing we saw when we pulled into the parking lot was the receptionist, dumping her stuff into her car and getting in. "Fuck him," she said when she saw me as she pulled out her keys. "I don't need this shit."

"What happened?" I asked her.

"He got fucking evicted!" she shouted, and drove away.

Olivia and I exchanged a glance. My stomach sank. Were Devon and Max too late? If Trent was evicted, I'd never see my money.

But when we walked into the building and up to the office, we found the door wide open, the front vestibule empty, and Trent's office occupied by two men: Devon Wilder and Max Reilly.

Max was sitting behind Trent's desk, frowning at his computer screen. Devon was lounging in a chair in the corner, looking through a sheaf of papers, but he looked up when we came into the doorway, his green eyes amused. "We've been busted," he said to Max.

I stared at the two of them in shock, but my gaze stopped inevitably on Max. He was wearing a black hooded sweatshirt, and his eyes were fixed on me. "What did you do?" I asked him.

"We evicted him," Max said.

"How?"

He shrugged. "Devon and I bought the building."

"We're the landlords now," Devon said, giving Olivia a wicked smile and returning to his papers. "This guy owes six months' back rent, so that means the premises are now ours. As well as everything inside them."

I crossed my arms over my chest. "Is that legal?"

"Let's ask Ben, my lawyer," Devon said, indicating his phone, which was sitting on the desk, obviously on speaker. "Ben, is this legal?"

Ben's voice came into the room. "You really wanna know?"

"Just keep Devon out of jail again," Max said to Ben's speaker. "He didn't get laid for two years."

"On it," Ben said.

I looked around, processing the idea that Candy Cane, Incorporated was no more. Next to me, my sister crossed her arms, her posture mimicking mine, and stared at Devon. "You two bought the whole building?" she said.

"It was cheap," Devon pointed out to her. "Though I

don't know what we're going to do with it now, because most of the renters have left and the location sucks."

"Let's get a pot dispensary for a tenant," Max said, tapping the keyboard in front of him. "They're legal now. We'll make more money than we know what to do with."

"Jesus, Max," Devon said. "You're a fucking genius."

Max hit a key, and the computer beeped. "Yeah, well, this guy's password was *password*, so next to him I definitely have a high fucking IQ."

"This is all very... satisfying," I admitted, "but how exactly does it get me the pay he owes me? And, I assume, all the other girls? If he's broke and he's evicted, he's probably leaving town. Which means goodbye, money."

Max looked away from the computer and at me. He looked hot this morning, his hair mussed, his beard trimmed from Friday night. "The money's already gone, Gwen," he said in his rough voice. "He's been spending it on something. The question is, what?"

"It doesn't help me if the money is spent," I argued.

Devon's voice was calm, and not unkind. "Don't worry about the money," he said, and I watched him exchange a look with Olivia. "You're Olivia's sister. It's going to be taken care of."

I opened my mouth to protest, and then I saw Olivia's face. She was staring daggers at me, and I knew she was going to make me take the money whether I wanted it or not. Shit. There was no denying that I was in a hole, and that the money would help. But it was hard to swallow. It made me feel like a loser, a failure. Now I understood why Max never talked about his five million dollars.

I looked back at Max and found he was looking at me

like he was reading my mind.

"What this is all about," Devon said, motioning to the office around him, oblivious to the storm of my emotions, "is shutting this guy down for good. If we just sue him, or pressure him, he goes underground and starts over again somewhere else."

There was a loud, breathy female gasp from the computer, followed by an orgasmic moan. We all stared as Max winced and clicked the mouse. "Jesus," he said. "This guy watches a lot of porn."

"I'm missing the good stuff," Ben complained over the phone. "Max, send me bank records, employee records, whatever you find. And the porn, but only the best ones."

"Get your own porn," Max said, closing the porn—presumably—and clicking around. "I found the list of all the girls who work for him, with contacts. I also found payroll records. We need to get in touch with every woman on the list. He's been skimming from all of them."

"What do we have here?" Devon said, pulling a sealed envelope from the stack of papers he was holding and tearing it open. "Oh, looky. A key."

"Jackpot," Max said. He yanked at one of the desk drawers, which didn't give. "Jeez, this guy is a real criminal mastermind."

Devon put the key in the drawer and opened it. I couldn't help it—I crowded behind him and stared inside, Olivia leaning over my shoulder. In the drawer were two white bricks, wrapped in clear plastic.

We were silent for a minute.

"There's your money," Max said.

"Oh, my God," Olivia said.

"What is it?" Ben said over the phone. "It's drugs, isn't it? Damn, I knew it. I should have bet money."

My head was spinning. "This isn't happening," I said. "Trent was buying drugs?"

Max picked up a pen from the desk and poked at one of the bricks without touching it. He slid it across the bottom of the drawer, assessing it from where he sat in his chair.

"What do you say, Max?" Devon's voice was quiet.

"Uncut, each one is worth fifteen grand, maybe twenty," Max said.

Devon pulled his keys from his pocket and spun them around his finger, his green eyes deep in calculation. "My guess is uncut," he said after a minute. "I'm thinking he got hold of a good connection, but he needed the money to get started. That, right there, is good shit."

"Porn and drugs?" Ben said over the speaker. "This guy is a walking party."

Max looked at me, his expression unreadable, and then he kicked the drawer closed with his toe. "He knows this is here," he said. "He's probably running right now."

"He is," Devon said, checking his phone. "He's on his way to LAX, based on the GPS I had put on his car last night. I'll make some calls." He put his keys back in his pocket and inhaled deeply, then smiled. "I love the smell of roasted drug dealer. This has been a productive day."

"Devon," I said, "thank you. And remind me never to piss you off."

He laughed. "You never met Cavan," he told me. "I'm the *nice* Wilder brother."

He left, and Olivia left with him, giving me a "call me later" sign over her shoulder. Ben hung up and Devon took his cell phone with him. And that left just me and Max.

He was still sitting behind the desk. He leaned back in Trent's chair, folding his hands smugly over his taut, flat stomach.

"I suppose you think you're pretty smart," I said.

He grinned at me, and then the chair creaked as he stood up. He came around the desk and pressed me to the doorjamb.

"Feel better?" he asked.

I could feel his heat through our clothes everywhere he pressed into me. I could smell that he'd showered this morning. But I hadn't seen him since the night he spanked me, and I wasn't about to give in so easily. "I'm still broke," I pointed out.

"Not for long."

"I have no job," I said.

"You'll think of something."

I shrugged, the motion creating friction between us. "I suppose there's some… satisfaction in knowing that Trent is going to jail," I admitted.

Max smiled. It was a wolfish smile, almost cocky, like I'd never seen from him before, and it was unbearably hot. This was not the Max I knew. This Max was bolder, cockier, ready to take what he wanted.

"You're welcome," he said. Then he kissed me, long and deep, his touch possessive and unmistakable.

He broke off slowly, and his fingers brushed my jaw. "No one messes with you," he said. "Ever."

I stared at him, my knees melting quietly to jelly.

"I'll be home around six," he said. "I'm going to cook dinner. There will be enough food for two. Join me if you want."

"I don't know," I said. "My ass still stings."

His eyes went dark and intense. "You can yell at me about that," he said. "Yell at me about whatever you want. It's up to you."

"I'll think about it," I said. "You'll find out what I decide at six."

"Right," he said. "See you later, Gwen."

Chapter 18

Max

D R. WELDMAN LISTENED IN HIS USUAL SILENCE, BUT when I finished he actually sounded impressed. "Max," he said, "it may be unorthodox, but you're making progress."

I stared at the wall, the same as I usually did. "Maybe," I admitted. "I feel different."

"Interesting. How so?"

It took a minute for me to put my finger on it, but finally I did. "The fear," I said. "It doesn't seem so bad."

He scratched on his notepad. I always wondered what he wrote on that thing. "That's encouraging. I notice you didn't say that the fear had gone away."

"The fear will never go away." I already knew that. I'd lived with it since the second I'd seen the wall of fire blast over the windshield of our SUV outside Kandahar. "You can't kill fear. At least, I can't. But I'm tired of it. I've let it run me for four years. I'm finally done."

Dr. Weldman made another note. "So you helped your girlfriend with her job situation."

I flinched. I'd felt so fucking good, doing that for Gwen—making her problem go away. I'd nearly devoured her on the spot, except that it would be weird and sort of creepy to fuck her in her ex-boss's office. But it didn't leave us any further ahead than we'd been before. She was still her. I was still me. "She's not my girlfriend," I replied. Not that I knew of, anyway.

"Pardon me. The woman you've been seeing."

I turned and gave him a glare. Therapists never said anything by mistake, ever. "You're an asshole, you know that?"

He gave me a bland look and shrugged. "It seems like a serious thing to do for someone, to buy a building in order to get her boss arrested for the drugs he's been dealing."

"I suppose," I said. I hadn't told Dr. Weldman about the spanking; I'd finally decided there was something even the guy who regularly looked inside my head shouldn't know. "It isn't that I'm not serious about her. I'm serious about fucking everything. It's that I don't know whether she's serious about me."

"That may take time," he allowed.

"I'm fine with that," I said. "I'm not going anywhere. But I'm in it now. All in. If she isn't—if she really isn't—then I've lost. That's something I keep coming back to."

"You've done a lot of hard work, Max," Dr. Weldman said. "Your strength has to come from within, not from another person."

"That's true." I turned and looked at the wall again. "But sometimes another person makes you want to be better."

"Is that what's happening?" he asked.

I thought about that. I thought about the rest of the five

million dollars I still had in the bank. And suddenly I had the beginnings of an idea of what to do with it.

And the thought didn't scare me.

"Yes," I said. "I think it is."

The money I'd been sitting on, pretending it didn't exist—the change that had seemed so big I couldn't take it in all at once. I could see it now. I could handle it. I could even make the best of it, make something that hadn't been before. And in a strange, crazy way, that was all to do with Gwen.

I wanted to do things for her, but it wasn't only that. I wanted to do things for myself, to make myself better, so I'd deserve her. She challenged me, she turned my world upside down, she made me rethink everything. She never treated me with pity or fear. She made me remember all the good things I'd thought before the IED happened, all the things I'd wanted to do. I wanted to do them now, except now I had a reason. And now I had a plan.

Maybe it wouldn't work. Maybe I'd fail. It was possible. And it didn't matter.

Because I wasn't quitting. And finally, I realized, there was something I could do.

Chapter 19

Gwen

WHO WAS I KIDDING? I SHOWED UP FOR DINNER. He made pasta with grilled chicken and vegetables. I was surprised at how good it was, and then I wasn't. Max had the best body of any man I'd ever seen. He was obviously not a guy who ate a lot of takeout pizza.

I'd thought long and hard about what to wear, and ended up in a jersey dress and ankle boots, my legs bare, my hair down. Some guy catcalled me when I got out of my car at Shady Oaks, and I didn't even mind. I felt sexy. There was a difference between the sexy feeling of wearing a tiny cowgirl outfit and the sexy feeling of being on your way to get—hopefully—laid by a big, burly, bearded animal with a skill at orgasms and a serious lack of manners. At twenty-six, I was just learning this for the first time. And I was much, *much* preferring the second kind of sexy.

The day was still spinning through my head. Everything had changed so completely in a few hours. Candy Cane was gone, my career as a stripper was over, and I was unemployed, but I didn't have to worry about money, at least for the short term. And most of that was because of Max Reilly.

Max. What the hell were we doing? What did I even want us to be doing? What did he want? He had a confirmed bachelor's life, living alone in his apartment and going to his gym and his bar. I had a single girl's life, working and dating and never getting serious. The fact was that when we met, neither of us was looking for anything serious. Neither of us had been looking for anything at all. And since that explosive first hour we were together, I had no idea where I wanted this to go.

Maybe he didn't, either. Maybe he just liked some hot sex after four long years.

But he'd *bought a building*. As a gesture, it left getting a woman flowers far in the dust. Yet Devon had bought the building, too. Maybe they'd both done it out of a sense of duty to Olivia's sister, as well as outrage over what Trent had done and the need they both seemed to have to raise shit, especially for lowlifes like Trent. They'd both seemed to have a good time putting him under.

Maybe, for Max, it hadn't really had to do with me.

He was so ridiculously hard to read. I could stare into those dark eyes, into that dark frowny face behind its sexy beard, and have no idea whether he was mad at me, about to fuck me, or thinking about something else entirely. And words—well, he didn't have many of those either. I'd always dated men who could talk all night, usually about themselves. I'd never dated a man who used words so sparingly. But I liked it. It meant that whenever Max said something, he meant it.

No one messes with you. Ever.

Oh, yes. He'd meant that.

"Your boss got arrested," he told me, continuing the Max pattern as he put a bottle of wine between us and sat down across from me at his little table. "It's done."

"So that's it?" I asked. "Trent is toast?"

He shrugged. "Pretty much."

I bit back a grin and grabbed the wine bottle, pouring us each a glass. "A funny thing happened to me this afternoon," I said. "A courier showed up with an envelope. It was a check for all of the back pay I was owed, plus an extra five thousand dollars."

Max put his fork in his pasta and stirred it. "I think that's a severance payment," he said. "Devon was talking about that. He paid all of the other girls who got ripped off, too, by the way. Not just you. With a severance for each of them."

I sipped my wine and stared at him. He was wearing his usual jeans and a white t-shirt with a dark blue flannel shirt buttoned over it. He wasn't as dressed as he'd been the other night at the theater, but still he looked like he'd made... an effort. A Max-type effort. His hair was neat, not mussed for once. He'd traded his black zip-up sweatshirt for something with buttons. It was possible the shirt was even new.

Some rich guys impressed women by taking them on private jets; Max did it by changing his shirt. And I still felt touched, because I got it. I understood. I wanted to unbutton that shirt and pull his clothes off and explore every inch of his body until he was changing his shirt a hundred times a day, just for me.

Instead I took a bite of pasta, which was delicious. "Well, here's the interesting thing," I said. "I cashed my check, and then I went to my landlord's office to pay the back rent I owe. And I found that not only was it already paid, but my next six months' rent is paid in advance as well." I swallowed another bite and raised my eyebrows at him. "Or maybe you already know that part of the story?"

Max grabbed his wineglass and frowned at me. "That building isn't very safe," he grumbled. "I went in there and said I wanted to pay your rent, and he didn't even ask who the hell I was. I could have been anyone."

I licked a drop of wine off my lip. "My sugar daddy," I teased.

That made him grumble harder. "You know that's not it. You just need a few months to figure out what's next, that's all."

"And I don't have to sleep with you?" I batted my lashes at him. I wouldn't tease him so much if he didn't make it so easy.

He took a gulp of his wine. "I told you before, fuck me or don't fuck me. It's up to you."

I pressed my knees together under the table as a pulse of excitement made its way up my body. "I pick option A," I said.

He stared at me for a long moment, and then he laughed softly. "We can do that if you want. You want me to spank you again?"

Jesus. I tried to stay casual and not stare longingly at the bedroom door, a few feet away. "That was rude," I told him. "Spanking me like that."

Max put his fork down. "You think?"

"Uncouth," I said, stirring the last few noodles on my plate. "Ill mannered."

His voice was rough. "Yeah?"

"Brutal," I said, the words making the pulse of excitement run through my body again. I put down my own fork. "Forceful. Powerful." I raised my gaze to his. "Rough."

His eyes were dark on mine. He shoved back his chair and stood. "Come here."

I was out of my chair before I could think. He took my wrist—a little roughly, just like I wanted—and took me into the bedroom, which was dark except for the light spilling in from the main room. I had kicked off my shoes before I even hit the doorway, and when he pulled me into the room I eagerly got on the bed.

No negotiation. No finesse. No seduction. I was drunk with anticipation, wet and ready. I felt free and totally wild, my dress sliding up my bare thighs as I leaned back on my elbows and looked up at him. He watched me in the dim light, and I felt like the sexiest woman in the world.

"Take your shirt off," I told him.

He reached down and grabbed my ankle, holding my foot in midair. "You think I'm just going to do what you want?" he said.

I tugged my foot, but he didn't let go. His big fingers were wrapped around my ankle, his muscled arm holding me easily. It was a game, one that made my breath come short. "Do it," I said.

He grabbed my other ankle, so now he held both of them, my legs slightly spread and held in midair. "Maybe I won't," he said. "You're bossy, even after I spanked you. Maybe I'll just fuck you with my clothes on."

Oh, I could play this game. "Take them off or you don't fuck me at all," I countered. I lifted my skirt up, showing him my panties between my opened legs. "I'll walk out of here, and I'll take this"—I slid my hand down into my panties, over my pussy—"with me."

His eyes followed my fingers, almost as if he couldn't stop himself, as my fingers moved beneath the fabric. Then he let my ankles go and unbuttoned the blue shirt, pulling it off. The t-shirt followed next.

I kept my hand moving. "Now your pants," I said.

He unbuckled his belt and dropped them, like he'd done in his living room that day. He was wearing black boxer briefs. I couldn't see his damaged leg from my angle, but I didn't forget about it, that he'd said he'd rather not wear it in bed. "Your leg," I said.

He hesitated for a fraction of a moment, but when I nodded, he sat on the edge of the bed and took it off. He did it quickly; I hadn't seen exactly how the leg came on and off yet, but it didn't seem to be complicated. I heard the leg thump to the floor.

Then he turned and crawled up the bed toward me, his big shoulders and arms rippling. His look was intent. "Your underwear," I said.

"Nope," he replied, arriving between my knees. He pushed them apart, hooked his fingers in the sides of my panties, and ripped them off, yanking them down and away in one smooth motion. I was left bare beneath my skirt, my hand over my pussy. He lifted my hand in his and put my fingers in his mouth, tasting them.

"Oh," I said.

He finished that and dropped my hand again, pressing himself higher between my thighs. "I owe you one," he growled. "Now lie still until you come."

He dropped his head, putting his mouth on me. It felt so good I closed my eyes and stretched back, my hands over my head, my hips lifting. His beard scratched my bare skin, tickled the insides of my thighs. He tasted every inch of me, exploring, licking and sucking just right, and the world spun away. I came fast and hard, like my body was in a rush, my back arching against the mattress. I'd never come so fast, or so often, with any other man—or even on my own. This was what he did to me.

He pushed my dress up, and I helped him pull it off over my head, tossing it away. I unhooked my bra and tossed it, too. He kissed my neck while I hooked my fingers in the waist of his boxer briefs and tried clumsily to push them down.

"You want it?" he said against my skin.

I had nothing but honesty. "Yes."

He turned me over, and I propped my elbows in the sheets. I heard him shove the boxer briefs down. His big hand positioned my hip and he slid deep inside me from behind.

I dropped my forehead and closed my eyes. Why did this feel so good with him, and only him? This was a little like our first time on his sofa, but the angle was different, deeper, his touch gentler. He moved the hand from my hip and cupped my pussy from the front with it, his palm pressing into me as he moved.

"Oh, my God," I said.

I felt his teeth graze my shoulder. "So fucking loud when I fuck you," he said. "Spread your legs for me, Gwen. Wider."

I did, and he angled deeper, moving in rhythm with me.

I gave myself up to it, the sensation from the front, from behind, from his body moving over mine, his mouth against my shoulder, my breasts brushing against the cool sheets.

It was wild and soft at the same time, sweet and hard. "You make me insane, you know that?" Max rasped against my neck as we moved. "I'm losing my fucking mind."

I couldn't answer, because I was coming again, this time in a slow spiral that went on and on as he kept moving in me, as his hand still held me. And then he went still and I felt him release, his sigh harsh against my skin.

My eyes stung suddenly, and I pressed my face into the sheets, fighting a crazy, unreasonable urge to cry. I didn't know what was happening to me. I didn't know what person I was going to be tomorrow, or in an hour. I didn't know what I was doing.

All I knew was that I didn't want it to end.

Chapter 20

Max

GWEN SEEMED RESTLESS. SHE CLEANED UP IN THE bathroom for a long time, splashing the water, as I dozed in my post-orgasm haze. I should have been thinking something coherent, but I wasn't. I was just a mass of satisfied testosterone.

The mattress moved as she got in bed again, but she didn't lie down. I pulled out of my doze when her hand touched my damaged knee. "I want to see your leg," she said.

My eyes opened and I felt my body tense. She was sitting near the foot of the bed, naked, her gaze on my fucked-up leg, studying it in the near-dark. Her fingers were already running over my skin, gently exploring. I felt my jaw tighten, my teeth clench, but it was too late and I wasn't about to push her off. I stayed still.

"So many scars," she said, touching the side of my thigh, the back where the flesh had been torn.

I forced myself to look at her. Her body was utterly beautiful, her breasts round and full, her skin flawless, her waist a perfect curve. Her lashes were lowered over her blue eyes as she looked down at me, and her lovely mouth was set in a line of concentration. "Most of the scars are from the explosion," I explained. "Some of them are from the surgeries."

She explored higher up my thigh, which of course interested my dick, even though we'd just finished and I was quietly freaking out. Then she explored back down again, below my knee to where my leg ended. "Does it hurt?" she asked.

"Not much anymore. I get phantom pain sometimes. I lost some of the hearing in my right ear from the blast—the doctors say thirty per cent or so. And I have to stretch my leg regularly or the muscles bunch up."

"They bunch up? Where?" She grabbed the thick muscle just above my knee and squeezed it, kneading. "Here? This feels tight."

I was silent for a long minute, completely unable to speak.

"What?" Gwen asked, lifting her hand. "Did that hurt? My God, I'm so sorry."

"Do that again," I managed.

She dropped her hand to the same spot and dug into the muscle, her hand surprisingly strong. "Here?"

I made a noise. Starbursts of pleasure were bursting in my leg, traveling up into the rest of my body. "Holy *shit.*"

She laughed. "I guess that means I'm doing it right." She kept going, using both hands now, squeezing the big muscle and down into what was left of my calf. "Jeez, Max, these are hard as iron. You could get a massage, you know."

"No fucking way," I choked, the response automatic. I didn't want anyone except doctors to see my leg, and certainly not to touch it. I did the stretches and massaged it myself sometimes. But if Gwen would do this for me, she could touch my leg anytime she wanted, discomfort be damned.

No woman, no lover, had seen me as I was since the explosion happened. Until Gwen.

And it was fantastic. "I'll buy you another building," I moaned as she moved to the inside of my knee, and up again. "I'll buy you a goddamn city block."

"That's what they all say," she said. She shifted on the mattress, getting a better angle. "Devon said you had a girlfriend. Before you got injured."

What? Between the sex and the massage, I was too blissed out at first to follow the change in conversation. I felt myself frowning. "Why the hell did Devon tell you that?"

"Is it true?" she asked, still squeezing me. I couldn't read her voice.

"I suppose." Shit, I hadn't thought about Jackie in years. "She was in nursing school."

"Was it serious?"

I raised my head and looked down at her, but her hair was falling in her face as she looked down, and she wasn't looking at me. "What the hell is this about?"

"I'm just curious." She glanced at me, her expression carefully blank. She shrugged tightly and went back to kneading my muscles.

I tried to answer the question through my fuzzy thoughts. "To be honest, we didn't see each other all that much. She was in nursing school, and I was usually deployed."

"So it was mostly sex, then," she said.

"What? Not really, no." The penny dropped. "Wait a minute. Are you jealous?"

"I didn't say that."

"You are." I watched the tense line of her shoulders. "You really are."

She raised her head and looked at me, pushing her hair back from her eyes with one hand. Her gaze was fiery. "I don't like the idea of anyone else touching you," she said.

I laughed. "Gwen, I really don't want any fucking details, but you're hardly a nun."

She made a dismissive noise and flipped her hand. "Amateurs, all of them," she said. "Boring."

Jesus, she was full of herself. Still, that was flattering. "Well, stop worrying," I told her. "Jackie and I broke up during my last leave. She didn't cheat on me, but she'd met some other guy she wanted to be with, and I couldn't even care. We split and I went back to Afghanistan. I haven't seen her since." Had that only been four years ago? It felt like a century, something that had happened to some other man. If I saw the Max Reilly from that last leave on the street, I probably wouldn't even recognize him.

"All right," she said, apparently satisfied. She stopped her massage and rose up on her knees, looking down at me. "Well," she said, her voice dropping sexily as she saw what was going on between my legs. "You're awake."

"You're in my bed," I said, putting my hands on her hips and moving her up. "Trust me, I'm awake."

She settled over me and rubbed lazily over my cock, leaning forward and bracing her arms on the bed. "Um," she said, a purr of pleasure as she moved again. "Oh God, that's nice."

"You're wet," I said, pressing her down.

"Mm," she said again. Her voice was a lazy drawl now,

and I knew the feeling. I had no idea how this woman made me feel better than I did with anyone else, how she made it so easy. How my body knew hers so well. I only knew that I didn't like the idea of anyone else touching her either. Anyone but me.

I kissed the side of her neck and moved her so she was on my cock, lowering her down on me. She made a sweet little noise as she did it, and then she moved in a slow circle.

This. Being connected with another person. Being this close. I'd never thought I'd feel this—not ever. I'd thought I was done.

I moved my hands up and cupped her breasts, touching them gently. We were going slower this time, easier. The game from earlier was over.

I moved one hand to her spine and stroked downward, toward the delicious flare of her hips and her ass. "Amateurs, huh?" I said.

Her voice was fuzzy, lost in what she was doing. "What?"

"Amateurs," I said again, my hand sliding lower, lower. "It's a shame. But I guess you finally got to ride a man who knows what he's doing."

When my finger dipped low, she tensed for a second, then ground back against it, curious. She leaned down so her breath teased my lips. "I like that," she said. "Do you think you can make me come?"

"I'll do my best," I said. "Hold on and we'll see."

Chapter 21

Gwen

"I FEEL DIFFERENT," I SAID.

Olivia raised her eyebrows at me. We were in a small Chilean restaurant around the corner from the small art gallery on Market Street where she worked as a graphic designer, creating all of the gallery's brochures, maps, and guides. "You look the same," she said. "Except you're not wearing any makeup, and I've never seen you eat so many empanadas before."

"Holy shit, these are good," I said, grabbing another one. Score one for me: I didn't have to worry about lunch bloating my tummy, because I didn't have any gigs later. Or ever again. It was a little hard to do a convincingly sexy act with a stomach full of deep fried dough. "I do feel different, though," I insisted. "Did you feel different after you met Devon?"

Her eyes widened, and then she shrugged. "Well, you know I had a crush on him for months before I met him."

"True." Devon had lived across the way from Olivia's Shady Oaks apartment, and she used to watch him from her window, totally sick with lust. "But after you met him, though."

She bit an empanada and chewed thoughtfully. "The short answer is that everything changed when I met Devon. Like, literally everything. Starting with the sex."

That made me think of me and Max in his bed five days ago. And then me and Max when he'd come over two days ago and we'd done it on my table. And in my bed. And in my shower. And on my floor—twice. Holy shit. "Do you remember the dolls we played with growing up?" I asked Olivia.

"Sure."

"We had Barbies, but then we had that knockoff doll who was supposed to be a Barbie, but wasn't."

"I remember her," Olivia said. "She kept falling apart."

"Her legs fell off, and we used to put them back on her backwards," I said. "She'd have these awkward backward legs on. I've had so much sex in the past week that I feel like that doll, you know? Like someone took my legs off and put them back on the wrong way."

She had to put down her lunch, she was laughing so hard, her hand over her mouth as she bent over the table. "I don't want to say I know what that feels like, because I don't want to gross you out," she said, "but I totally know what that feels like."

I rolled my eyes. "Honey, I guessed." I hardly thought a beast like Devon Wilder would be shy in bed. He probably kept my sister plastered to the sheets half the time. "Looks like we're both getting properly laid now, huh? Though it happened in different ways."

"How serious are you two?" she asked, taking a drink

of her water. "I mean, Max seems like a pretty serious guy."

"Are you warning me not to break his heart?"

"You're sort of known for it, Gwen." She looked at me with a thoughtful, knowing sister's look. "But I think Max is different."

"He is." I put down the empanada I was holding and wiped my fingers on my napkin, dropping my gaze. "I told him about what happened when I was eighteen."

She was quiet, and I looked up to find all the humor gone from her expression. "Are you serious?"

"Yes." I took a breath. "I feel like—I feel like what happened has maybe been holding me back all these years."

Olivia put her glass down. "Oh, Gwen."

"I know you think I got over it," I explained. "The pregnancy, the miscarriage, all of that. I know I gave you and Mom that idea. But I didn't. I really didn't."

"I know," she said.

I stared at her.

"I believed you at first," she said. "It was over, and you seemed to move on. You tried acting school, and you flunked out, but you brushed it off. I didn't think that meant anything, because I flunked out of art school at the same time."

I bit my lip. Our mother, an actress who had starred in a successful sitcom in the late eighties and early nineties, had put together some of her residuals and sent us both to school—me for acting, Olivia for art. We'd both failed. Now, after years as a graphic designer, Olivia had found her way back to art, working at a gallery and doing her own art in her spare time. But acting wasn't my passion; I'd thought I'd be good at it, because I was pretty and outgoing, and it had seemed like something to do. Neither was a good enough reason to pursue such a hard career.

"When you got the stripping job," Olivia continued, "I started to wonder. You seemed... tough. Hard. But we'd been apart for a few years by then. I thought maybe that was just how you were. The pregnancy was so long ago, and you never mentioned it, never mentioned the father again. You didn't seem to be heartbroken over him."

"Not him," I said. "I was never heartbroken over him."

She looked at me. "But the experience was painful."

I stared unseeing at the busy, crowded restaurant behind her shoulder for a minute, and then I said, "Stripping was my way of making sure nothing ever hurt me again."

"Oh," she said. She looked upset. "I let you down as a sister, didn't I? You could have talked to me anytime. I would have listened."

I reached out and put my hand on hers. "You didn't let me down. I didn't want to talk. I couldn't even admit to myself that there was anything to talk about."

We were quiet for a minute, both of us absorbing that. Then she said, "And now?"

"I feel better," I told her honestly. "Max made me realize what I've been doing." He'd had to spank it out of me, but it was still true. "I don't know how he knew myself better than I did, but he did."

"And he helped you get out of the business, even if he had to buy a building to do it," Olivia said. "You didn't answer my question. Do you think you two are serious?"

I opened my mouth to answer, then closed it again. Opened it, then closed it, like an idiot. I didn't know the answer. It hadn't been very long; I'd never been serious about anyone before; I didn't know how he felt about me, not really. But at the same time, I hadn't been lying when I'd told him that I didn't like the idea of another woman touching him. If any woman even looked at Max sideways, I'd probably go *Dynasty* on her. But did that mean I was serious, or just a possessive bitch?

Because I could totally see myself as a possessive bitch.

"You're thinking about it," Olivia said. "Admit it."

This was getting too serious, so I said, "I'm thinking about fucking him. That's different."

But my sister, damn her, wasn't fooled. She just smiled and picked up an empanada. "You're so full of shit," she said. "Eat your lunch."

* * *

I texted Max as I left the restaurant. *What are you doing?*

Talking to my therapist, he texted back.

Jesus. Max was texting during a therapy session? I'd never been in therapy, but I had to guess that was frowned on. *Stop it,* I wrote. *Talk to you later.*

There was a pause. *We're not in a session,* Max wrote. *Just talking.*

That made me frown as I got in my car. He was just... hanging out with his psychiatrist? That didn't sound normal, either. His psychiatrist was a man—I remembered that from the conversations we'd had during the bouts of exhaustion in our sex marathon. But Max hadn't mentioned they had a social relationship.

I decided I'd ask him about it later, since he was in the middle of the conversation, whatever it was.

I drove home, my mind wandering as I drove, thinking about throwing out some of my stripper clothes and making room in my closet. Thinking about calling my mother. Thinking about taking college courses—what kind of courses could I take? The array of choices was overwhelming. I didn't want anything to do with acting or performing, but I liked being with people. Maybe sales, or marketing, or PR. Or event planning. They had courses in that, right?

I was still deep in thought as I pulled into the underground parking lot beneath my apartment building. It was afternoon on a weekday, and the underground lot was deserted, filled with cars but no people. I parked in my designated spot and got out, keys in hand, when I caught something from the corner of my eye. Someone coming my way on foot.

I turned to see who it was.

And that was when everything fell to pieces.

Chapter 22

Max

I T HAD TAKEN SOME CONVINCING TO GET DR. WELDMAN
to meet me outside our usual sessions, but he'd finally
agreed. Why, I had no idea, since it was probably
completely against his rules. But I'd asked, and he'd agreed,
as long as the conversation was not going to be about my
mental health. I promised him it wasn't.

We met at a tiny sandwich shop near his office, where an
old Polish man stood behind the counter, grumpily making
sandwiches with his bare hands. I had no idea what was on
mine—it was spicy and vinegary and had some kind of meat
in it—but I didn't care. Being nervous made me hungry.

"Okay," Dr. Weldman said. "Tell me whatever is on your
mind. Before I lose my license to practice."

I put down my sandwich. I was terrible at this shit, so
I said the first words I could get out. "I have five million
dollars."

He didn't drop his lunch. "That's nice, Max," he said.
"But you told me that already. What does it have to do with
me?"

"I'm not saying it right," I said. "My friend Devon inherited a lot of money. I told you that. He inherited a billion dollars. And he knew I had hospital bills, and my dad's debts, so he gave me some money. More than I need."

Dr. Weldman watched me thoughtfully, not stopping me even though we'd been over this in one of our sessions. "Go on."

"I told him I didn't want all that money," I said. "That I don't need it. And he said something that has stuck with me. He told me that if I didn't want all that money, I should give it to some other veteran to pay *his* bills with."

"A nice gesture," Dr. Weldman said.

"It was just something Devon said," I explained, "but lately I've been thinking about that idea. That I could pay other guys' bills—to see you, for example. Some guy who needs help but can't afford it, like me a few weeks ago. I could use my money and get him help instead."

Finally he put down his sandwich. "That is a very kind thing to do," he said, picking his words gently, "but I don't see how we could do it. My patient information is strictly confidential, as you can imagine. I can't just send you other people's bills."

"I know," I said. "That's why I want to set up something official through the clinic. Like an official charity." I pushed aside my plate and picked up the salt shaker. "So let's say this is a veteran," I said. "He has PTSD and he needs help, but he can't afford it. He puts in an application." I set the salt shaker down and picked up the pepper. "This is a doctor, like you. Not just you, though. Ideally we'd have a network of doctors who are interested and qualified. We'd start out in the Bay Area and, if it works, we'd expand out."

I put down the pepper shaker a few inches from the salt. "This is my organization," I said, picking up a spoon. "It connects the guy from this half"—I put the handle next to the salt—"to the guy from this half." I put the bowl of the spoon next to the pepper. "We find the right guy for the right patient. He gets help. And we pay the bill."

Dr. Weldman looked at my salt-spoon-pepper outline for a minute, thinking. "It's simple on the surface, but in reality it isn't. You're right, the clinic management would have to be involved. They'd have to be enthusiastic, in fact. We'd have to balance transparency with patient confidentiality. And when you bring in insurance companies and veterans' benefits, it all becomes complicated."

"But worth doing," I said. "Right?"

He looked at my setup some more. "It's certainly worth doing," he said. "There are many veterans who could benefit from a service like this. But my own influence only goes so far. You'd have to go up the food chain, Max."

"That's why I'm starting with you," I told him. "Get me a meeting with your boss. Or better yet, his boss."

Dr. Weldman sighed. "I can try. I've never known a patient to propose something like this before. I have no idea what they'll do, if they'll take you seriously."

"I'm always fucking serious," I said.

He smiled a little. "I know you are. In fact, I know you quite well. When you propose something, you always mean it with everything you have. It's why I agreed to meet with you in the first place."

"Because you knew I wouldn't waste your time?"

"Because I knew whatever you had to say would be

interesting," he said, "so I wanted to hear it. I'll make some calls. But you'll have to sell this thing, Max. The people who can put this in motion are suits, not just doctors. You'll have to put together a more formal presentation than this." He motioned to the salt and pepper shakers. "They'll want to see proposed financials. Projections. And although five million dollars is a lot of money, it's finite. If you give it all away, eventually this project ends."

I could feel my frustration growing. He was right, but it didn't make it any easier to hear. "I know my money will run out," I said. "We'd raise donations. Maybe get corporate donors."

He nodded. "It's a valid plan. I'm just saying that the people you need to talk to will need to see it laid out. They'll need to be convinced." His voice gentled. "You have to be ready."

I stared at my salt-spoon-pepper diagram. I knew what he was saying—I'd just spent four years fighting PTSD and anxiety, and here I was, proposing something that was probably going to cause me the maximum anxiety possible. Meetings, suits, proposals. Having to talk. To sell.

I felt that. Every single shitty, terrifying part of it. But I looked at the salt, the spoon, and the pepper, and wondered: if I didn't do this, what the fuck was I doing with my life? James, David, and Keishon had died in that IED attack—I had their names tattooed on my arm. They'd died, and I'd come home. What the hell was the fucking point?

I looked up at Dr. Weldman. "I'm ready," I said. "But I'm not wearing a fucking suit. If they can't handle a guy in a t-shirt, then fuck them. I'll find some other way."

* * *

I was feeling pretty good when I left the sandwich place and got in my car. Like maybe I could actually do this. And the first person I wanted to talk to was Gwen.

I hadn't told her about my plans yet. I told myself it was because I wasn't sure I was going to do it, but that wasn't true. I just wanted it to sound... good by the time I told her about it. Real. Like something that could be a success.

Because her opinion mattered. She mattered. To me, she mattered more than anything. Without her, I was done.

I was walking to my car, my leg feeling good, when my phone rang in my pocket. I pulled it out and saw that it was Ben, Devon's lawyer. "Hey," I said when I answered. "What's going on?"

His voice was tight, urgent. "Max, we have a problem."

Immediately my gut tightened. "What problem?"

"This Trent Wallace guy. He just made bail half an hour ago."

I stopped still, next to the driver's side door of my car. "What do you mean, he made bail?"

"Someone must have posted it for him. Fuck, I don't know. I thought he didn't have any money. The fact is, he paid his bail. He's free."

Something hot and cold was climbing up my spine. Something was wrong. Very wrong. "Okay. So what the fuck is the problem?"

"You know that GPS I had installed on his car?" Ben said. "It's still there. He never found it. So I'm tracking him right now. And the first place he went when he got out was

Gwen's apartment building."

My vision went red for a second, then cleared again. I was in war mode, like I'd been for four years in Afghanistan. "If he touches her, he's fucking dead. I'm on my way."

"Wait," Ben said. "He's already on the move again. That's what I'm calling to tell you."

"What the fuck do you mean?"

"I mean that he drove to Gwen's building, and then he left again. And Gwen isn't picking up her phone."

I popped open my door and slid inside, positioning my leg. "Tell me where I'm going," I said, putting the phone on speaker and dropping it on the seat next to me.

"He's on the move," Ben said. "He just got on the freeway." He gave me coordinates, and then he said, "I've already called Devon. He might call the cops."

"I don't give a fuck about cops," I said, meaning it. "They can come, or they can stay. Just follow him, and keep talking." Then I started my car, and drove.

Chapter 23

Gwen

TRENT LOOKED TERRIBLE. HIS DYED BLACK HAIR WAS
sticking up and frizzy, and his face was extra pasty,
with dark bags under his eyes. He was wearing an
oversized long-sleeve shirt with the sleeves rolled up and a
huge, dark brown stain on the front. I was too grossed out
and terrified to want to know what it was.

He'd grabbed me in the parking lot, thrown me into his
passenger seat, put a hand on my throat, and told me that if I
made a sound, he'd kill me. I'd tried to scream and fight him
off, but he'd punched me in the stomach, one hit that was
so hard I'd nearly thrown up. When I could breathe again
and see through the tears streaming down my face, he had
started the car and was driving.

I'd had some plan in the back of my mind that I could
start screaming and call the cops, but the first thing Trent
did was grab my phone and drop it on the floor of the driver's seat, slamming his heel into it again and again. "Shut up,
for God's sake!" he'd shouted at me, his voice cracking.

My hands were shaking. Gone was the smug, smarmy

Trent I'd always known as the owner of Candy Cane. This man was pale and desperate and mean. To make things worse, it started to rain as we drove, the rain pelting the roof of the car.

"Listen," he said as he pulled onto the freeway, the wipers moving frantically. "Just shut up and listen, all right? I'm not going to hurt you. Not if you do what I say."

I curled my hands over my aching stomach and watched the freeway fly by. God, I couldn't even jump out of the car. I took a deep breath and tried not to panic. Maybe if I could keep him talking, I could figure out a way to escape. He couldn't stay on the freeway forever.

"What do you want?" I said.

"That was a shitty move your boyfriend pulled," Trent spat. "Doing me in like that. I was in the middle of a deal. A big one. I just needed some cash to pull it off. Now it's all over."

"Fuck you, Trent." I shouldn't say that—I knew that. I shouldn't provoke him. But fuck him—just fuck him. "You want me to have sympathy because you were using my money for your drug deal?"

"Shut up," he said again. "Jesus, you always were a mouthy bitch. You think you're better than everyone else. Well, you're not. You couldn't just keep it quiet until I did the deal, could you? And the party—you couldn't just work that without making a stink? It was important."

"Wait a minute," I said. "That party was for your *drug dealing* buddies? You wanted me to do a show for them?"

"I wanted you to fuck them," he said bluntly. "That would have been helpful, Gwen. I owed them money. Now I owe them even more."

"I think I'm going to be sick," I said.

"You better not," he warned. "It was your boyfriend's dick move that got you here, and now you're going to pay."

I tried not to let on how those words terrified me. Trent could probably smell fear, like a dog. "What do you want?" I said again.

"It's simple," Trent said, as if there were anything simple about this situation. "I need money. A lot of money, to pay back the people I owe for this busted deal, or I'm dead. I've got it on good authority that your boyfriend has a lot of fucking money, even though you wouldn't know it. So, since he's the one who got me into this shithole, he can pay to get me out. Or it's you who gets hurt."

Oh, no. This wasn't going to work. Trent didn't know who he was dealing with. "It's you who's going to get hurt," I told Trent. "He's going to kill you."

"You think I'm scared of some guy with a fake leg?"

That made me angry. "He got that fake leg in *Afghanistan* you piece of shit," I yelled at him, "serving his country and kicking ass. You think a guy like that is going to think twice about doing you serious damage?"

"You're not listening," Trent said. "He'll have to think twice, or it's going to go bad for you."

"Then he'll just hurt you *harder*, you idiot," I said.

"Nobody has to get hurt if he pays me!" Trent shouted, his voice ringing through the car. "So shut up! Just shut up! This will work! It has to!"

I was afraid he would hit me again, so I was quiet after that. We were crossing the San Mateo bridge in the rain. I had to think of a way out of this. He had to stop the car sometime, and when he did I had to find a way to scream, get attention, get someone to call the cops. Trent wasn't armed that I could see. I glanced down at the ballet flats I was wearing with my jeans. I was strong and fit, unlike him. If I caught him by surprise, how far and how fast could I run?

He took an exit and pulled into an industrial complex somewhere south of Oakland, a massive area that looked like it belonged to a pharmaceutical company. He parked at the back of the huge parking lot, which was mostly empty, surrounded by nothing but other parking lots and faraway buildings, with the freeway in the distance beyond, shrouded by rain. I was just trying to calculate how far I had to run to get help when Trent pulled out his phone.

"Okay," he said. "You're going to call loverboy. You're going to tell him I have you, and that if he doesn't bring one hundred thousand dollars to the location I give you, I'm going to start punching your pretty face."

I stared at him. "What the hell happened to you?" I asked.

"I had the opportunity to make a big buy," Trent said. "A real connection in the business. But I needed cash. Who cares if a bunch of strippers aren't getting paid? Seriously? Everyone knows you're all a bunch of fucking sluts. Like one of you could afford a lawyer?" He looked disgusted. "If you could afford a lawyer, you wouldn't be stripping in the first place. That's how it works."

"So you took our money," I said.

"I had to." He shrugged. "They gave me the merchandise, but I couldn't sell it right away. I thought I had a buyer, but he got cold feet and backed out. But I still needed to pay the guys who'd given me the product." He stared at me, his eyes bloodshot and cold. "Then your boyfriend came along and sunk the whole thing, and the cops took the product. And the guys I owe say that's not their problem. They say it's mine." My gazed darted past him out the window, and he shook his head. "Don't think about it, Gwen. I'll catch you if it's the last thing I do. I'll run you over if I have to. I'm about to be killed here. You don't understand how desperate I am."

The phone. That was my only play. He wanted me to call Max, tell Max to meet him. I had no doubt that if I made that call, Max would come. Except he'd bring a different kind of deal than Trent thought he was making.

"Fine," I said, holding out my hand. "I'll call Max. I'll tell him whatever you say."

Still he held on to the phone, his pasty face looking in to mine. "You do it, or you'll get another punch in the stomach. And this one will break a rib."

I gritted my teeth. I was getting tired of his threats. I wanted to hear Max's voice more than anything in that moment, wanted to know he was coming for me. "Give me the phone," I said.

But still he held on to it, as if he hadn't quite thought it through. As if he was just realizing that I could take the phone and dial 911 just as easily as I could dial Max. *This guy is a real criminal mastermind,* Max had said. He definitely had desperation more than brains on his side.

"Okay, listen," he said, stalling for time. "There's a location where he has to meet me with the money. It's a warehouse in Oakland. He has to come alone and bring one hundred thousand dollars. No backup, no cops. You get it?"

"Just tell me the address and give me the phone."

Trent opened his mouth, but then something happened.

A car pulled up next to ours. Trent was turned in the driver's seat, facing me, and he barely had time to turn before a huge, muscled arm ripped open the door and dragged him out onto the concrete.

Trent made a high-pitched *whoop* sound, as if he was on a particularly painful roller coaster. He fell backward, propelled by an arm that had a familiar tattoo on it.

"Max!" I shouted, scrambling out of the passenger door and running around the car. Max had Trent on his back on the ground, looming over him, his big hands fisted in Trent's jacket. They were both getting soaked, and so was I as the cold rain pounded down over me. I could see the muscles of Max's back like granite beneath the cotton of his t-shirt. He was face to face with Trent, and I had never seen Max's face so cold, so angry, or so utterly murderous.

"Did you hurt her?" he roared.

Trent gasped something unintelligible, and Max lifted him and slammed him back against the pavement, once, hard.

"*Did you hurt her?*" he roared again.

"Max!" I shouted, but he didn't hear me. I didn't want to touch him—I wasn't sure he even knew I was there. He was so focused on Trent, I wasn't sure he saw anything else.

"Fuck you, Reilly!" Trent finally managed to shout. He was squirming now, kicking his legs, probably trying to kick Max's bad leg out from under him. "You fucked me over! I was going to pay them back—"

Max lifted him again and slammed him down, and this time I heard Trent's head thud against the pavement. In the distance, police sirens were approaching.

"*Did you hurt her?*" Max shouted a third time, rain

dripping from his face, his hair.

"Jesus!" Trent said, sagging in Max's grip. "It was just one hit! It was nothing! You're fucking crazy, you piece of shit!"

Max went very still. I watched his expression change. It was a little like watching coal go white-hot—it may not be visibly burning, but you know it's deadly to touch. His brow cleared, and his eyes glittered. In his position, crouched over Trent, I could see the veins bulging in his flexed arms, the perfect tension in his big body. He went deep inside himself, right there before my eyes, went deep inside his head and saw something no one else could see. He put one hand around Trent's throat, pinning him to the ground and pressing. Trent squirmed and made a strangled sound. The moment held on a knife's blade.

"Max," I said.

This time he heard me. He blinked, and I watched him slowly come out of himself, though he didn't remove his hand from Trent's neck. The police sirens were coming closer. "Gwen," he said—just that one word, said in a low growl, but I knew it wasn't a curse. It was a plea.

I came toward him and put a hand on his shoulder. The muscles were bunched like rocks. "You should let him go," I said. "The cops are coming. I'm fine."

He angled his head slightly toward me, but he didn't turn. "Is it true he hit you?"

I didn't look at Trent, who was starting to struggle to breathe. My stomach was sore, and I couldn't take a deep breath. But I said, "I'm okay."

Max knew that was a yes, and for a second his big hand squeezed harder. His voice, when he spoke, was low and dangerous. "I should fucking kill you," he said to Trent.

The police cars pulled in to the parking lot, their lights flashing. They stopped and a door slammed.

"Max," I said again, squeezing his shoulder.

"Stand up, sir," I heard one of the cops say. "Right now."

"It's over," I said softly, so only Max could hear. "Let him go."

He did. He relaxed his hand from Trent's throat and lifted it. He stood. He looked me up and down, his dark eyes unreadable. And then, without saying a word, he looked away.

Chapter 24

Max

T HEY DIDN'T ARREST ME. THEY TOOK ME TO THE station and questioned me, but they didn't arrest me. It seemed that after everything, Trent Wallace didn't want to press charges for assault.

Gwen, however, pressed every charge against Trent that she could get her hands on. Abduction. Assault. Threatening her. She went to the hospital, where she had a report done on the injury to her stomach, and the cops took pictures. I wanted to tell her that she was my fucking superhero in those few hours, but I couldn't. Because I was stuck in an interview room.

What is your relationship with Miss Maplethorpe? What is your relationship with Mr. Wallace? You claim you've never met him. How is it that you're the new co-owner of the building where he rents an office, and you evicted him a week ago?

For fuck's sake, just let me go. Just let me get back to her. Just let me go.

Devon sent Ben to sit in the interviews with me, just in case, and Devon himself was waiting in the police station when they let me go. He was sitting in a hard chair, wearing jeans and an old gray t-shirt under a zip-up sweatshirt, a pair of motorcycle boots on his feet. Despite being a billionaire, he looked right at home with the drug dealers, pimps, and hookers coming and going through the station, and not one of them looked at him twice.

"You done?" he asked when I stood in front of him, pulling on my own sweatshirt.

I shrugged. Ben had gone home already, taking off in his beat-up Civic, his day's work done.

Devon stood up. "I'll take you back to your car."

I didn't want to go back to that parking lot, where I'd had one of the most disastrous moments of my life, but I had no choice. My car was still there. I'd come here in the back of a police cruiser.

I was tempted to feel shame at that. I'd grown up on the streets of LA, and it was only through determination and strength of will that I'd avoided getting caught up in the criminal life. It was tempting and so easy to do. But I'd always kept my nose clean, and I'd enlisted to get myself away from those kinds of temptations. The fact that my life would end up going to shit worse than if I'd stayed home was not something I predicted. And now, at twenty-nine, I'd had my first ride in the back of a cop car.

But I couldn't feel ashamed. Devon was my best friend after all, and he'd done time—time he'd deserved for the crime he did. Like him, I couldn't see how else it could have gone. If I had it to do over again, I'd still pull Trent Wallace out of that fucking car, cops or not, and I'd still put my hands around his throat. In fact, if I had to do it again, I'd probably squeeze harder.

So no, I didn't feel shame. But guilt—that was different. Guilt was something I had a lot of.

Olivia was with Gwen, Devon explained to me, staying with her while she dealt with cops and doctors and making sure she got home okay. Since Gwen's phone had been smashed by Trent, she was out of contact, except through Olivia.

"You should go see her," Devon told me as we drove back south of Oakland and headed for my car. "Olivia says she's at home. She's shaken up, but calm."

I looked out the window. "I don't think that's a good idea."

"Maybe you should let Gwen decide that."

I looked at him. I was in no mood for a lecture, even from my best friend. "You know this is my fault, right?"

Devon shook his head. "I knew you were going to say that."

"I was going to say it because it's true. If I'd stayed the hell out of Gwen's business, if we'd never bought that building and pushed Trent Wallace into a corner, none of this would have happened."

"So what were you supposed to do?" Devon asked. "Let him keep stealing from your girl?"

I paused at the words *your girl*, realizing that I'd never thought of Gwen that way, but it felt right all the same. She probably had a different idea. "There were other ways I could have handled it."

"Sure," Devon said. "Let him off the hook. Let him skate. Leave him free to go steal from and scare and coerce other women instead. You could have done that."

"Gwen wouldn't have gotten hurt," I argued.

"Or she would have," Devon said, calm and implacable. Devon was always calm, except when it came to Olivia. "Maybe, when he learned about your money, he would have hurt her anyway in a play to blackmail you, and it would have turned out the same. You ever think of that?"

I glared at him, uselessly since he was staring ahead at the road. "Fuck, you're a philosopher now?"

"I've gotten wise," he said, pissing me off. "I've had to. Listen, Max, you're smart, and you've always had balls. We both know it. But having money just means your balls have to get bigger and your smarts have to get smarter. That's what I've learned since inheriting. You make a call, you follow through, and you deal with the consequences, whatever they are. That's how you have to live."

I scratched my beard slowly. "I'm giving my money away," I told him.

"Oh yeah?" He didn't even sound angry. "To who?"

"Other veterans. Does that count as having balls?"

"Yes. And what happens when the money is gone?"

I thought I didn't know the answer, but I did. It came straight from my gut. "Then I'll raise another five, and give it away. And another. And another. I don't give a fuck how long it takes. I'll do it until I'm dead."

Devon was silent for a second. "You tell Gwen any of this?"

"No." I looked out the window again.

"Think about it," Devon said.

I made my gaze stay out the window. I made myself say the words, though in the end it was easy. "I love her a lot."

He let the words hang there. "I got that part," he said. "I've known you a long time. But it's better if you tell her."

"I'm shit for her," I said.

We were in the parking lot, pulling up next to my car. "Yeah, well," Devon said. "Like I say, maybe you should let her decide that."

I got out, pulling my keys from my pocket. Fuck, my leg hurt. It had been a long day. "Thanks for the ride," I told Devon.

He rolled down his window as I circled my car. "Go see her," he said, and drove off.

I opened my car door and got in the driver's seat, and then I stopped. With the door still open and one leg on the ground. I ran a hand through my hair and stared at the wet parking lot, at nothing.

It was dark now. Late. She was probably asleep.

She wouldn't want to see me.

I had two choices. Go home to Shady Oaks, or take my chances with Gwen.

I sat in the dark for a long time, wondering which one I would do.

Chapter 25

Gwen

OLIVIA STAYED WITH ME THROUGH EVERYTHING. Through the police statement, and the hospital exam, and the other police statement, and the review of the police statement. Trent was arrested, with no chance of bail this time, since his assault on me had violated his bail in the first place.

While we waited in a hospital corridor, we called our mother on Olivia's phone and filled her in. When Olivia passed the phone to me, my mother was crying.

"Oh, sweetie," she said, her voice choked with tears. "Tell me you're okay. Please tell me you're okay."

I hadn't cried until that moment, but suddenly I lost it. It was the familiar sound of my mother's voice, distorted with panic and love for me. Tears ran down my face. Why had I ever thought my mother didn't care?

"I'm okay, Mom," I choked out.

"That awful job," she said. "I hated it so much. I worried about you every day. I'm coming to see you. I'm getting in the car right now."

I mopped the tears from my face. Mom lived in LA. She was the opposite of the cliché of the Hollywood has-been—she was a good mother, kind and loving, with her head on straight. But still, all those years in Hollywood had left her in a gentle bubble, a place where too much reality hit her harder than other people. She would probably just flutter around me, helpless and more distressed than I was. "Don't come, Mom," I said. "Olivia's here. I'm just bruised, that's all."

"The doctors have checked you out?"

"Yes. I'll be all right in a few days, I promise."

"No more stripping," Mom said. "I mean it. Find something else to do—anything. I'll help you if you need it. But no more."

I sighed, sniffing. I hadn't known my job had worried her so much. "I was already quitting. And I am going to find something else to do." I tried to break it to her gently. "It won't be acting, though, Mom. Sorry."

"Oh, goodness, sweetheart, you don't have to be an actress!" I'd upset her all over again. "I just sent you to acting school because that was what you said you wanted. And you're so beautiful. But acting is a terrible career. It's full of misery. Go find something that makes you happy."

Olivia handed me a Kleenex, and I mopped my face. "I love you, Mom," I said.

"I love you too, Gwennie."

Strangely, considering we were sitting in a hospital hallway after my drug dealing boss had kidnapped and assaulted me, I hung up feeling better than I had in months, maybe years. Mom hadn't called me Gwennie since I was a little kid—she was the only person who ever called me that.

Hearing her say it made my heart crack open. I handed the phone back to Liv, and she put her arm around my shoulders, hugging me to her. We sat like that, content and quiet, until the doctor said I could go.

Now, hours later, I was home in my apartment. I'd had a shower—delicately avoiding my bruised stomach—and something to eat. I put on a pair of girl boxer shorts and a cami. I lay in bed for a while, thinking I would sleep and not sleeping. Finally I got up, covered up in a robe, and sat restlessly on the sofa, wondering what to do. I had no phone, so I couldn't call anyone. I was just about to resort to flipping aimlessly through TV channels when there was a soft knock at my door.

I stood up, but I didn't open the door. "Who is it?" I asked.

"It's Max," a familiar voice said.

My heart did a crazy flip in my chest, and I realized I wanted to see him. That I'd wanted to see him for hours. I opened the door, and we looked at each other. He was wearing the same jeans and black hooded sweatshirt he'd been wearing hours ago, when he'd pulled Trent out of the car.

His hair was mussed. He looked tired. His eyes held mine, and for once he wasn't frowning. He just looked worried and quietly vulnerable.

He leaned one shoulder against the doorframe, since I hadn't stood back to let him in yet. "Sorry," he said. "I couldn't call."

I swallowed. I could still see him opening the door and pulling Trent backward, out onto the pavement. I could still see him crouched over Trent, shaking him, shouting, his hands on Trent's neck. I could still see Max's face, so unlike the Max I knew.

That Max was gone. In his place was this man, who simply looked at me like he wanted me. I knew, just like I knew my own name, what it had cost him to come here. What it was still costing him.

Maybe I should have been angry at him. Or afraid of him. But I looked at him and realized I just loved him instead.

"Come in," I said, stepping aside.

He closed the door softly behind him. "How are you?" he asked, his voice rough.

I shrugged and gave him the truth, tired of using the word *fine*. "My stomach hurts," I said. "It'll bruise, and then it'll heal. I cried once, when my mother called me. I didn't throw up. I can't sleep."

He ran a hand through his hair, mussing it further, and sighed. "Fuck, Gwen, I'm sorry."

"You're sorry?" I crossed my arms over my chest and looked at him. "For which thing, Max? For kicking Trent's ass when he abducted me? Or for getting me out of the stupid situation I'd gotten myself into in the first place?"

"Gwen." He shook his head. "This was my fault, and you know it."

"It's Trent's fault," I said. Just the thought of Trent's pasty face made me wish I could hit it, even though I knew he was in deep shit right now. "He made his choices. So did I when I decided to work for him, to keep working for him. Because I was too blind to see what the job was doing to me."

That made him frown for the first time. "Maybe. But that doesn't change the fact that since you met me, I've managed to screw everything up for you."

"What are you saying, Max?" I said. "Are you saying that we should never have met? Is that it?"

He looked at the ceiling, like he did when he was choosing his words. "In the overall scheme of things, it probably would have been best," he said. "But there's nothing that can be done about it now. I've already fucked up your life."

God, I was crazy about him. I wanted to smack him and yell at him and kiss him and climb him like a tree. No one made me insane like Max did. "So why are you here, then?" I managed to say. "If we shouldn't be happening at all?"

"Because I don't care," he replied. He came toward me, and I could see in his gait that his leg was bothering him. I wasn't about to demean what I'd just been through, but he'd lived through a fucking *explosion*. This man was the definition of courage.

He put his hands gently on my face and looked down at me, his thumbs on my cheeks. "I don't care," he said again. "I'm messed up, and I'm pissy half the time, and I'm not even whole. I'm bad for you. I'm the very worst. And I'm still not leaving."

"Good," I said, fighting back the emotion in my voice. "Don't you dare."

His face was stark with pain and want. "I'm wrecking your life," he warned me again.

I put my hands over his. "It needed wrecking, you dope."

"And you've sort of wrecked mine."

"I think you'll live."

He kissed me, slow and sweet and tender, and it was exactly what I wanted. It was sexy, but there was no rush; for the first time, we took our time.

Still, I dropped my robe and pulled him on to the bed. I

tossed away my top while he pulled off my shorts. He trailed his fingers lightly over my tender stomach, the touch feather-light, as he looked at it closely. Then he moved down, lifted one of my legs, and kissed the skin on the inside of my knee, his beard scratching me. His hand massaged my calf while kissed his way up the inside of my thigh, stopping just high enough, and then he switched to the other leg and did the same.

I relaxed into the pillows. I wanted him—I always wanted him—but I also wanted to be touched. After the day I'd had, I wanted him to touch me with kindness, with tenderness, with care. And somehow, like he always did, he knew exactly what I wanted.

He paused to unzip his sweatshirt and toss it off, then he picked up my leg again, his muscles moving beneath his t-shirt.

"Max?" I said, watching him.

He made a noise against my skin.

"What you did today was badass."

He stopped kissing me to shake his head. "You're bloodthirsty."

"Maybe I am."

"What would you have done if I didn't show up?"

"I was planning to kick him in the balls, then use his phone to call 911."

He smiled. "That's my woman," he said, and bent to kiss the inside of my thigh.

My woman. I liked that. He finished with my thighs, without touching between them, and moved up to my breasts, cupping one and caressing it, then bending to put his mouth on it.

Suddenly, I was all business. I pulled up his shirt, making him stop to take it off before he bent to my other breast. I slid my hand down his stomach to his belt, undoing it. He left my breast and braced himself over me, kissing me deeply as I undid his jeans and rubbed my palm over him. We rocked there for a moment, kissing, my hand moving slowly over him.

Finally he broke away, making a little noise of frustration. "Okay," he said. "This part takes a minute. Get used to it. You have to wait."

So I waited while he dealt with his shoes, then his jeans and boxers, and finally his leg. When he came back to me he was gloriously naked, just like I liked him.

He braced himself over me and kissed me again, and then he said, "I don't want to hurt you."

I bit my lip. He couldn't lie on top of me—he was way too heavy—but I didn't feel like being on top either. "We'll have to get creative," I said.

So we worked it out. We put a pillow under my ass, which raised my hips at just the right angle, and he braced himself over me on his elbows, both of us moving to get the position just right. It was worth it. When he thrust inside me, big and heavy, I moaned against the skin of his neck.

"Fuck," he said softly, and started to move.

Still, we went slow. I wrapped my legs high around his hips and locked my ankles behind his back, which made him groan. He was deeper like this, and I reveled in the feeling of him, taking his time.

I was just feeling that delicious burn deep inside me when he leaned back and withdrew. "*Max*," I complained.

He laughed softly. "I like to watch you," he said, and he

touched me, moving his fingers, his thumb, in just the right way. I pressed up into his hand and the feeling climbed, and just as I came—just as the sensation overtook me—he leaned forward again and thrust in to me, feeling me squeeze him. He fucked me through my orgasm, as it went on and on, his hips pressing him deep and hard into me as I twisted beneath him. I heard him hitch a breath and he came, his muscled arms shaking with the strain as he tried not to collapse on me.

Afterward we lay curled together on my bed. When he rolled onto his back, I moved on to my side, throwing a possessive arm over his chest and burying my face in the side of his neck, where I bit his skin.

"Ouch," he said. "I guess I should tell you something."

"You have a lineup of women you do this with," I guessed, nipping him again.

"Ouch. No. I'm probably not going to be rich for very long. I'm giving my money away to other veterans."

I propped myself up on an elbow and looked down at him. "You what?"

"I'm going to create a charity where vets with PTSD get counseling, and I pay the bill." He scratched his beard. "If it works out, I'll spend all my money on it, and then I'll raise more."

I stared at him, surprised. "When did this happen?"

"It hasn't happened yet. My doctor is going to set up a meeting with the bigwigs at the clinic so we can set up something official. I'll have to pitch them the idea."

He looked a little tense, and I knew exactly why. "You mean you'll have to talk. To sell them."

"If I even get the meeting. But yes. I'll have to sell

them… something."

An idea started forming in my head. I was quiet so long that Max finally said, "What?"

"I don't care if you're not rich," I told him. "Get your meeting. I think I know how we can give your money away."

Chapter 26

Max

TRUE TO MY WORD, I WORE JEANS TO THE MEETING. I just couldn't do the suit thing. But I matched the jeans with a white button-down shirt and a jacket that Gwen took me shopping for. I also got a haircut and trimmed my beard again, with Gwen in attendance, giving the barber directions. She looked at the end result and said it looked good.

The meeting was with Dr. George Tiernan, who was the head of the network of clinics mine was a part of—Dr. Weldman obviously had more influence than he thought he did. His office was downtown, right by North Beach, with Coit Tower looking down at us from the top of Telegraph Hill. I felt completely fucking out of place, but it was just one meeting. I could get through it. I had a plan.

Gwen walked next to me as I entered the building, bumping my shoulder with hers. "Ready?" she asked.

"Sure," I said. I even had a leather bag with file folders in it. Inside the file folders were the pages outlining how my proposed charity would work, including proof of my government and IRS non-profit paperwork. Three weeks of work in one small briefcase.

Gwen was wearing a demure dark pencil skirt that skimmed her knees, heels, a buttoned blouse, and a fitted sweater. Her blonde hair was styled—she'd done something or other with a curling iron—and she had makeup on. She looked smart and businesslike, but she also managed to look like a dirty fantasy at the same time. Or maybe that was just to me.

George Tiernan was in his late forties, a slim, fit man with that salt-and-pepper hair women love. He wore no wedding ring and his eyes lit up with pleasant surprise when Gwen shook his hand. She took no notice.

"It's so nice to meet you," she said. "I'm Gwen Maplethorpe, Head of Fundraising and Public Relations for Real Heroes. This is Max Reilly, Real Heroes' founder and president."

The smile he gave her—and, by extension, me—was genuine, and he shook my hand warmly. "It's a pleasure to meet you two. Please sit down."

Head of Fundraising and Public Relations. That had been Gwen's idea. *But that isn't a real job,* I'd said. Her reply was, *How the hell does he know it isn't a job? I'll have it printed on a business card.* The card she handed George Tiernan right now. He took it and nodded without a single question.

It worked. I took the papers from my briefcase, and we laid them out on the desk, going through everything. Tiernan asked questions—sometimes of me, and sometimes of Gwen. I answered pretty well, but when I went silent or got stuck, Gwen simply stepped in. She smiled at him. She made light jokes and laughed at his. She talked up the idea.

In short, she sold it.

She was a natural. Tiernan thought he was talking to a seasoned PR professional who had been doing the job for years, not a former stripper who had just started a night course. She made it look like this half-assed idea, that I'd first pitched to my PTSD therapist with a spoon and a couple of shakers, was detailed and well thought out. The idea was mine, but she gave it a polish I could never have given it in a hundred years.

It didn't hurt that she was fucking gorgeous. It wasn't lost on Tiernan, either, not by a long shot. He had no idea Gwen was anything more to me than an employee, and he was practically staring while trying to stay professional. He was under her spell. He was distinguished, classy, well-heeled—probably the kind of guy Gwen should be with. But I didn't give a fuck. She was mine.

"I'll certainly review all of this," he said toward the end of the meeting, when we'd laid it out for him. "But I'd like to know something from you, Mr. Reilly." He turned to me. "What motivates you to do this?"

I frowned at him. "What do you mean?"

"I mean, I know you're a veteran. But this is a big commitment, and a lot of money. Frankly, if it works out, it will likely take over your life." He looked at me more closely than he had for the entire meeting. "Why this? Why now? Why do it at all?"

It sounded like one of Dr. Weldman's bullshit questions, and I remembered that this guy was a doctor—likely a therapist himself. So I thought about it, and then I looked him in the eye.

"In the Marines," I said, "they taught us that if you're

in a dangerous situation—say, a burning building—you get yourself out. But they also taught us that if you're capable of getting yourself out of a situation like that, if you aren't injured and you're able to run, then you're capable of reaching back and pulling out the guy behind you. And the guy behind him. And the guy behind him. If you can save yourself, the chances are you can save someone else. Maybe more than one."

The room was quiet. Tiernan listened, his eyes on me.

"They don't teach us what to do after we come home," I said. "They leave you to figure it out for yourself. But I'm still a Marine in my head. I spent the four years since I've been home pulling myself out of my own personal burning building. And now I'm well enough that I can start pulling out the other guys. The guys who are still there." I shrugged. "That's the reason, I guess."

No one said anything at first. Tiernan sat back in his chair. I risked a look at Gwen. She was staring at me, lips parted, eyes wide. She looked speechless.

"Well," Tiernan said at last. "That's a heartfelt answer. I'll have to go over the logistics with a few of the other departments, like Finance and Legal, but I hope we can work something out."

With that, he dismissed me and turned back to Gwen, smiling again. She seemed to come out of her stupor and chatted back as they wrapped up the meeting. She didn't even react when he gave her his card with his personal cell phone written on the back—"in case you have any questions, any at all." She just put the card in her purse as we stood to go.

We were silent as we left the building and rounded it to

the small parking lot. I was suddenly exhausted. I reached the car first and tossed the briefcase into the back seat, then shrugged out of my jacket and tossed it in as well. Gwen still didn't speak.

I turned and looked at her. She was standing there, watching me, the breeze lifting her hair from her shoulders. She was staring at me like she had something to say.

"Just say it," I said, my voice tired. "You can go ahead. He's a nice guy. Good-looking. A doctor. Easy to talk to. Has a good job. He even wears a suit, and he probably didn't make anyone else pick it out for him. He always knows the right thing to say, and he gave you his number."

"I love you," she said.

I stared at her, stunned.

"I love you," she said again, "and I want—I want everything. I want marriage and babies and a home. A life. And I want this." She gestured to the building we just left. "I want Real Heroes to be real, and I want to be part of it. I don't want a fake job description for a single meeting. I want to help you build it. I want it to be true." I opened my mouth to say something, but she kept talking. "If you don't want those things, you have to tell me now, because I don't know what I'll do. I've spent eight years not wanting anything. Telling myself I it was too risky. And now, after all that time, I want *everything*. With you."

My heart had stopped. I could smell the ocean on the breeze that blew through the parking lot.

"I love you too," I said. She made a little sound, quickly choked off, her knuckles white where she gripped her purse. Jesus. She wanted kids? I'd give her as many as she told me to. "I want all that stuff," I said. "I do. You're the only woman

I want it with. I can't imagine it with anyone else."

"You mean it?" she said.

"I fucking mean it," I told her, stepping forward. She came into my arms and I pulled her close, feeling her breathe against me. She dropped her purse and put her arms around my waist, grabbing me tight as I smelled the pretty smell of her hair.

"I don't want his stupid number," she said against my shoulder.

"Okay," I said, leaning down and kissing the side of her neck. "We'll throw it out." I kissed her again. "You were amazing in there."

"Thank you." She sniffed lightly. "So were you. You're always amazing, Max."

"If you say so." I lifted her chin and kissed her mouth, slow and sweet. She parted her lips and the kiss deepened. Fuck, I loved kissing Gwen. I did it so long that someone passing on the street saw us and shouted, "Get a room!"

I broke the kiss and touched my lips to the soft line of her jaw. "That's an idea," I said.

"What?" she said, her voice trembling a little.

"I'm still rich for a while longer," I said. "Let's go to San Francisco's nicest hotel and get their nicest suite. Order room service. Take the rest of the day off in their nicest bed."

She sighed. Then she leaned up and kissed me one more time. My Gwen.

"You're the boss," she said. "Let's go."

Chapter 27

Max - Three months later

WE WERE BOTH ASLEEP WHEN THE PHONE RANG. Gwen was sprawled over me in our big bed, her arm slung over my chest, one long leg hooked over mine. It didn't bother me. I slept like a rock when I slept with Gwen.

But I woke up first and rolled over, reaching for my cell phone on the bedside table. I had finally left Shady Oaks, and Gwen had left her tiny apartment, and this was our place now—a modest condo in a low-rise building on the edge of Golden Gate Park. It wasn't big, but we didn't need much. We both liked the city, and I wasn't a fan of stairs anyway. It was home.

"Um," Gwen said as I grabbed the phone. I didn't recognize the number, and it was after midnight, but I answered it anyway. "Hello?"

"Max?"

The voice was familiar. Very familiar.

"Yeah?" I said.

"It's me."

Oh, fuck. I hadn't heard this voice in over a decade, but it was definitely familiar.

"Cavan?" I said.

Behind me, Gwen woke all the way up, her body tensing in surprise.

"Yeah," Cavan Wilder said. "It's me."

Devon's brother. Jesus. The last time I'd seen him was right after their mother had been murdered by her abusive boyfriend. The three of us had been living in LA at the time, where we all grew up together. Devon and Cavan's father had split years before, and their mother had dated until she met the wrong guy, who murdered her one night when they had a fight. The guy was arrested for it immediately and was still on Death Row, but it had left Devon and Cavan without parents.

Cavan had been eighteen at the time, Devon sixteen. Instead of sticking around to take care of his brother, Cavan had left town, and neither Devon nor I had seen him since. We didn't even know where he was. It was me who had helped Devon in the years afterward to avoid the foster system and keep body and soul together.

And now here Cavan was, phoning me in the middle of the night out of nowhere.

I sat up in bed. "Cavan. Where the hell are you calling from?"

He paused for a second, and I thought I could hear either traffic or wind in the background. "I'm in Arizona," he said finally. "I'm not sure exactly where. It's a truck stop on the highway."

"Are you all right?"

"Sure," Cavan said. He sounded like the same guy I'd

known years ago, but his voice was older, wiser. Probably like mine. "I'm fine. Things are just weird right now. I read some crazy thing about an inheritance."

Devon's billion-dollar inheritance was partly Cavan's, assuming Cavan came out of hiding. Devon had hired private investigators to look for him, with no results yet. "Yeah," I said. "It's true. You should call Devon about it."

"I'm not calling Devon," Cavan said. "Not now."

"Why not? He wants to hear from you." Devon would be beside himself to hear that his brother was alive.

"I'm not," Cavan said again. "I'm calling you, Max. You're saying the money is for real?"

Fuck, did he need money? What for? "Yes, it's for real. But you have to claim it."

"You mean come to California."

"Yeah, I mean come to California." I kept my voice calm. "You should come here anyway, man. Your brother wants to see you."

"I really doubt that." Cavan sounded bitter. "Shit. This might be complicated. I'll see what I can do."

"Why is it complicated?" I asked. Behind me, Gwen had sat up and was listening. She knew from Olivia how badly Devon wanted to find his brother.

"There's a woman," Cavan tried to explain. "She's in trouble. I'm trying to help."

"You have a girlfriend? A wife?"

"No. She isn't my girlfriend. She's… I don't know what she is. Like I say, it's complicated. We can't come to California yet. I have to get her out of trouble first."

"Cavan, I don't get it. You aren't making sense."

"It won't take long," he said. "It's just a quick stop. And

then maybe we'll come. Or maybe I'll come alone. I don't really know. Just tell Devon that, okay? Tell him I'll come when I can."

"Cavan—"

"Tell him," Cavan said, and hung up.

I stared at the phone. The number he'd called from was there, but it was either a pay phone—if those still existed—or a burner. I knew it already.

Gwen put a hand on my shoulder. "Oh, my God," she said softly.

"I have to call Devon," I said. "Cavan Wilder is alive after all these years. And he's coming to California."

A Note From Julie

Thank you for reading *Dirty Sweet Wild*! *Rich Dirty Dangerous*, which is Cavan's story, is out now.

I was a dead man the minute I inked her.

I've spent ten years as the ink man for the Black Dog MC. When a member needs ink, he comes to me — and I always obey. Because even when you're not a brother, disobeying the Black Dog is deadly. So they own me.

And they also own her.

Dani. Beautiful, sweetly sensual, temptation incarnate. The president's woman — completely off-limits. But when she comes to me to get a tattoo, and begs me to get her out of the Black Dog before he kills her, my blood starts to burn for the first time in a decade. And when I realize my own reason for getting out — an inheritance from nowhere that will make me obscenely rich — I have to decide.

Stay, and we'll both be sacrificed.
Run, and we'll both have a price on our heads.
Take Dani, like she begs me to, and I might not live to see the morning.

Some things, I hear, are worth dying for.
Tonight is the night I find out.

Turn the page for an excerpt!

Chapter 1

Cavan

I WAS A DEAD MAN THE MINUTE I INKED HER. I KNEW IT from the first.

Her name was Danielle, Dani for short—no last names were used in the Black Dog Motorcycle Club—and she didn't even look twenty-five. A tall, slender body with long legs and narrow hips. Dark hair worn long and sleek down her back, arrow-straight, with a long fringe of bangs over her dark-lashed brown eyes. A real beauty, every inch of her, and one hundred per cent the property—yes, property—of the Black Dogs' current president, McMurphy. She wanted ink, and when the Black Dogs wanted ink, they came to me. Which meant I'd have to touch her.

I was a dead man.

She lay in my chair and handed me the drawing of what she wanted. Four small black birds, flying in silhouette; nicely drawn, and not too hard. "I've never had a tattoo before," she said, watching me from those dark eyes while McMurphy sat on the other side of her, his eyes fixed on me. "This is my first one."

Virgin skin, I thought. I didn't look at McMurphy.

"Did you draw these yourself?" I asked her.

She nodded.

Impressive. "Where do you want it done?"

She pulled up her t-shirt, exposing first a sweet, flat plane of stomach and then the underside of one breast in its lacy bra. "Here," she said, indicating the skin just below her breast. "And here." Her finger traced around the curve of her breast to the side.

I did look at McMurphy then. She was his property; I had to make sure he was permitting this. The idea of the president's woman picking out her own tattoo, and placing it on her own body, without the president's approval was unheard-of in the Black Dog MC. McMurphy's expression said that he already knew what she was going to propose. He kept his gaze fixed on me, his blue eyes in their sun-weathered face as hard as chips of diamond. "Just keep your hands where they belong, Wilder," was all he said.

It wasn't exactly my protocol to grope a woman's tits while I was inking her, but he had a point. The tattoo wasn't on her breast, but close enough that I'd have to touch it. My fingers brushing it. Quite a bit. I'd also have to look at it—I was already looking at it right now.

It was just a breast. Every woman had 'em—two, in fact. You could go on the internet and see as many as you wanted, on women doing whatever turned you on. Dani's weren't very big, maybe small B cups, fitted to her slender body. Which I should definitely not be thinking about.

I looked back at her to find her watching me. "It'll hurt," I warned her. "You've never done this, and the skin there is sensitive."

"I can take pain," she replied.

The words sat there for a second. Of course—any woman who was McMurphy's would have to be able to take pain.

"Okay," I said. "You're going to have to take your shirt and bra off, but I'll give you a sheet to cover yourself with."

She nodded. Over her head, McMurphy said, "How long will it take?"

I shrugged, looking at the drawing again. "An hour and a half maybe."

He fixed me with his laser gaze. "Do I have to sit here for an hour and a half and watch you, Wilder?"

"If you want," I said. It was best not to show fear to McMurphy; he ate it like candy. "It doesn't matter to me."

"You know the rules," he said. McMurphy was about forty, way too old for this woman, with a hard face and muscles like a bulldog's. He wore his beat-up leather cut, like he always did, and I could smell him from where I sat: sweat, oil, and yesterday's whiskey. Some women just couldn't resist it, like an aphrodisiac.

The rules meant that I wasn't supposed to touch the president's old lady. I wasn't supposed to touch anyone's old lady. I was just the guy who did the club's ink, not a full-fledged brother.

I looked him back, straight in the eye, and said, "How long have I been inking the Black D?" Which meant *Of course I know the rules, idiot.*

McMurphy shoved his chair back hard and stood up. If I'd flinched in that moment, he would probably have hit me, but I didn't.

"You touch her, you're dead," he said. "Fucking dead." He turned and left the room.

I looked back down at Dani. She hadn't even looked at McMurphy. She was still watching me. She still had her shirt hiked up, her skin showing, the edge of her bra visible. Her look wasn't hostile—it was afraid, but courageous. Her body was so vulnerable. In a few years, her eyes would be hard and her body would be a canvas of the hits she'd taken.

And I realized something. When he'd warned me not to touch her, McMurphy had assumed that it mattered, that I cared about dying.

And I didn't.

Made in the USA
Coppell, TX
30 June 2020